CLOSE CALL

Books by Lauraine Snelling

Hawaiian Sunrise

A Secret Refuge

Daughter of Twin Oaks

Red River of the North

An Untamed Land	*The Reapers' Song*
A New Day Rising	*Tender Mercies*
A Land to Call Home	*Blessing in Disguise*

High Hurdles

Olympic Dreams	*Storm Clouds*
DJ's Challenge	*Close Quarters*
Setting the Pace	*Moving Up*
Out of the Blue	*Letting Go*
Raising the Bar	

Golden Filly Series

The Race	*Shadow Over San Mateo*
Eagle's Wings	*Out of the Mist*
Go for the Glory	*Second Wind*
Kentucky Dreamer	*Close Call*
Call for Courage	*The Winner's Circle*

CLOSE CALL

LAURAINE SNELLING

BETHANY HOUSE PUBLISHERS
MINNEAPOLIS, MINNESOTA 55438

Close Call
Copyright © 1994
Lauraine Snelling

Cover by Dan Thornberg

Published by Bethany House Publishers
A Ministry of Bethany Fellowship International
11400 Hampshire Avenue South
Minneapolis, Minnesota 55438
www.bethanyhouse.com

Printed in the United States of America by
Bethany Press International, Minneapolis, Minnesota 55438

Library of Congress Cataloging-in-Publication Data

Snelling, Lauraine.
    Close call / Lauraine Snelling
       p.   cm. — (Golden filly series ; bk. 9)
    Summary: As Trish continues her horse racing successes and her struggles with her faith, she faces some mysterious, anonymous threats.

    [1. Horse racing—Fiction. 2. Christian life—Fiction.]
I. Title. II. Series: Snelling, Lauraine. Golden filly series ; bk. 9.
PZ7.S677C1   1994
[Fic]—dc20   94–27180
ISBN 1–55661–488–8 (trade paper)   CIP
                                              AC

To Elaine Aspelund
who shared her near-death experience
with me and who has been sharing
the special love, joy, and peace she found
with those around her
all her life.

LAURAINE SNELLING is a full-time writer who has authored a number of books, both fiction and non-fiction, as well as written articles for a wide range of magazines and weekly features for local newspapers. She also teaches writing courses and trains people in speaking skills. She and her husband, Wayne, have two grown children and make their home in California.

Her lifelong love of horses began at age five with a pony named Polly and continued with Silver, Kit, Rowdy, and her daughter's horse Cimeron, which starred in her first children's book *Tragedy on the Toutle*.

CHAPTER ONE

Winning races is better than—than, Trish Evanston struggled to think of anything better. Hot fudge sundaes . . . Miss Tee, the filly born on Trish's sixteenth birthday . . . riding her thoroughbred, Triple-Crown-winning colt, Spitfire—well that rated number one. No contest there. She waved again at the racing fans who'd packed Portland Meadows Race Track for the opening program.

A solid block of teenagers wearing crimson and gold, the colors of both Prairie High School and Runnin' On Farm, whistled and shouted back at her. Even her government teacher, Ms. Wainwright, whooped and hollered with the best of them.

On the edge of the winner's circle, Trish accepted the congratulations from the fans pressing in around her. "Well, winning the Hal Evanston Memorial Cup is not quite as big as winning the Triple Crown, but it's right up there." She grinned at the woman who asked the question. "Thanks for coming and for supporting racing in Portland."

Someone else handed her a program. "For my daughter, Becky. She's a real big fan of yours."

"Tell her hello for me." Trish signed the program and handed it back to the man.

"She wanted me to tell you how sorry she is your father died." The look on his face conveyed his own sorrow.

"Thank you. That means a lot." Trish shook his hand. "It really does."

"Trish!"

She looked up to see Doug Ramstead, all-American guy and Prairie High's quarterback, waiting his turn.

"Hi, Doug. I could hear you whistling above everybody."

He lifted her clear off the ground with a breath-snatching hug. "You were great, little one. I'm so proud of you." He set her back down and tapped the tip of her nose with his forefinger. "Now you just get the next two, okay?"

"I'll do my best." Trish watched the Big Man on Campus of Prairie High make his way through the crowd. No wonder half the girls were in love with him. He was just as nice as he was good-looking.

"Your father sure would be proud of you, Tee. I know, because I sure am." Trish's mother, Marge Evanston, put an arm around her daughter's shoulder.

"Thanks, Mom." Trish blinked a couple of times. So did Marge.

It was one of *those* moments—when her father seemed so close that she knew if she turned quickly enough, she'd see him standing right behind her, his face split by a smile to dim the sun. Hal Evanston had loved racing, but he'd loved his Lord even more—and was never afraid of telling the world so.

Trish vowed to always follow his example.

She followed the others out of the bronze and gold chrysanthemum-bordered winner's circle only to be confronted by a cluster of reporters, already shouting questions. She answered as best she could. "Yes, God willing, I'll be riding in the Breeder's Cup. Our filly Firefly will run in the Oaks the day before. No, I'm fine after all that mess over the Meadows. After all, they never shot right at me."

She tried to edge her way toward the jockey room, but the reporters refused to budge. "Yeah, I miss my dad every day but especially at times like this." She kept the thought *dumb question* from showing on her face. Finally she threw her hands in the air. "Hey, I've got another race to ride. How about we meet after I'm done and I'll answer any questions you have?"

They grumbled but good-naturedly backed away.

David walked beside her, back up the tunnel to the saddling paddock, and opened the gate so she could cross to the jockey rooms.

"Thanks, David. I thought you'd headed for the barn."

"Patrick and Brad can take care of that end. I just wanted to make sure you were all right."

Trish stopped and looked up at him. "Huh?"

"Well, with what's gone on and all—" He stopped and took a deep breath. "I worry about you, you know."

"Hey." Trish patted his chest. "That's Mom's job. She'd be the first to tell you."

David nodded, a rueful grin tugging at the corners of his wide mouth. "She gave up worrying, remember? I guess I just realized this world is full of kooks and I don't want them hurting my sister."

"It's over, David. And we're no worse for wear."

"Really?"

She could feel the depths of his caring clear to the center of her heart. "Really. God says He'll take care of us and He did." She started up the hall to the silks room, then stopped and turned. "It's over, brother of mine. All but the court stuff."

David nodded, but she could see the concern still reflected in his dark eyes.

He settled his Runnin' On Farm cap more firmly on his head and, with a flick-of-the-wrist wave, trotted off to the backside.

Trish headed once more to pick up Anderson's silks. How good David's caring felt! She was lucky to have a big brother like him.

"Some ride!" Genie Stokes raised her hand for a high-five. "Couldn't happen to a nicer person."

"Thanks. You didn't do so bad yourself. You ever seen a three-way photo finish before?"

Genie shook her head. "But then I haven't been in the winner's circle as much as you. I think that filly of yours just reached farther with her chin. Gotta get Patrick to teach me how to get my mounts to do that."

"Right. He keeps a secret book of tricks that he shares only with his friends." Trish pulled her helmet off and shook out her dark, shoulder-length hair while dropping the helmet on the bench and plunking down beside it. She waved and acknowledged the comments of the other women jockeys. Drawing in a deep breath of the steamy, liniment-scented air, she dropped her head forward and rotated her neck, then shoulders.

"Takes some reconditioning, doesn't it?" Genie sank down beside Trish after pulling her own silks over her head. She massaged her temples and up into her hair with her fingertips. "Man, no matter how much I work out, nothing is the same as riding in the races."

"I know."

A squall from the black box-speaker up in the corner cut into the locker-room buzz.

"We better get moving." Trish hung her silks on a hook and dragged the Anderson pink and gray colors over her head. "If I sit here much longer, I'll tighten up."

"Go ahead, see if I mind." Genie walked over to the long mirror and winked at Trish. "More for me that way."

"You want Gatesby?" Trish joined her at the counter, one eyebrow raised.

Genie shook her head. "He's still up to his old tricks, isn't he?"

"Let's just say I've learned to duck fast."

But Gatesby seemed on his best behavior when she joined Patrick, David, and owner John Anderson in the saddling paddock. The bay gelding stood calmly while Patrick tightened the racing saddle one last time. After Gatesby rubbed his forehead on her silks, the horse blew gently and tipped his head slightly for her to scratch his other ear.

When Trish looked at Patrick with a question, he just shrugged and shook his head. "He's feelin' up to snuff, waren't he, David?"

"Don't trust him for a minute." David glared at the animal in question. "He's just setting you up."

John Anderson conveniently stayed out of tooth range.

But when David gave Trish a leg up, the gelding pricked his ears and tossed his head. After pawing with one front hoof, he lifted his nose, snorting drops of moisture right in David's face.

"I know this horse hates me." David wiped his face with his sleeve. "Get him outa here, Tee."

The parade to post bugled across the grassy infield and echoed in the tunnel.

"Right." Trish chuckled again while Patrick led them out to the pony rider.

"Bless ye, lass." Patrick handed the lead to the pony rider and grinned up at her before stepping aside.

"Thanks." Trish patted Gatesby's deep red neck and would have leaned forward to hug him if they'd been at home. Even loving Gatesby was easy right now.

In fact, with the students chanting along the walkway, a race to run, and the light making her blink when they cleared the tunnel, loving the entire world was easy. As number one, they led the parade past the grandstands and back again.

"See, over there, fella?" Trish murmured in her horse-calming singsong. "Your owner is here to watch you for a change. You gotta do good for him." Gatesby danced from one side to the other, tugging against the lead. He snorted with each stride when they broke into a canter, strutting his stuff for the crowd.

Trish rose in her stirrups, glorying in the wind against her face and the powerful animal beneath her. "Yeah, this is your day, fella. I can just feel it."

Gatesby argued with the handlers for a moment when they started to lead him into the number one slot, pulling against the lead and swinging his rump to the side.

"Easy, easy," Trish sang to the twitching ears. "Watch him!"

The assistant clamped his hand down hard right under Gatesby's chin.

"Did he get you?"

The man gave her a rueful grin, rubbing his shoulder with his free hand. Having had his say, Gatesby walked into the stall as if he'd never dreamed of causing a ruckus.

"You rotten horse, you." Trish couldn't keep the chuckle out of her voice. "You just have to show off, don't you?"

Gatesby tossed his head and turned to look at the horse in the stall on his right.

"You should warn those guys about him," Genie Stokes said over the noise of horses and humans.

"Yeah, make him wear a name tag that says 'I bite.' " Trish patted Gatesby's neck one last time and settled herself for the break. The number seven horse had to be brought in a second time, giving Gatesby a few added seconds to settle down. He took in a deep breath, just like Trish, and let it all out.

"Okay!" the call came. A brief silence. Trish relaxed her clenched fists. The shot! The gates sprung open and with a mighty thrust they broke free.

Gatesby never liked being on the rail, so Trish let him set the pace as they thundered into the first turn. Halfway through, the horse running shoulder to shoulder with them crowded the turn and, in the instant between one breath and the next, slammed Gatesby against the rail.

Trish fought to keep his head up and at the same time remain in the saddle. With things happening too fast to think, only reflex actions saved her from catapulting over the rail.

At the same time all her senses were tuned to the horse beneath her, checking to see if he was injured. But Gatesby pulled against the reins, gaining his rhythm again and extending his stride.

The field now ran a furlong ahead of them.

Trish settled back to ride. Had the bump been intentional?

Gatesby stretched out, each stride carrying them closer to the solid wall of rumps in front of them. By halfway up the backstretch, the wall disappeared as tired horses fell back, giving Gatesby room to maneuver. He surged past the laggers as if they were pulled to a stop. Around the far turn he gained on two more.

Trish rode tight on his withers, head tucked, making herself as small as possible. Down the stretch he paced the second-place horse and drove past it.

"Give it all ya got, fella," Trish crooned in his ear. "You can do it, come on." Gatesby thundered on, stretched out so far he seemed to float above the ground. Nose to rump, even with the stirrup. The finish line loomed ahead.

Genie Stokes laid on the whip. Her horse surged— and faltered.

Neck and neck. Over the line.

Trish had no idea who won. "What a run, Gatesby! You did fantastic!" She looked over at Genie, who kept pace with her as they slowed their mounts down. Both girls shrugged and swapped grins.

The second photo finish of the day and the two jockeys had been contestants in the earlier one.

"I don't know how you did it," Genie said as they walked their horses in circles in front of the grandstand. "How far back did you fall?"

"I'm just grateful we didn't go down. That was a close one. I wonder if we should turn in a grievance." She flexed her fingers to help stop the quivering that stretched from her hands to her shoulders.

"Did you see what happened?"

"Not really."

Trish looked over the spectators at the fence to see her mother's frown. David and Patrick were striding across the track toward her. When she circled again, she looked at the scoreboard, recently painted for the new season and still flashing "photo finish."

She waved her whip at the Prairie students and patted Gatesby's sweaty neck one more time.

"And the winner of the ninth race today is number one, Gatesby, ridden by Trish Evanston, owned by John Anderson and trained by Patrick O'Hern."

"Congratulations." Genie vaulted to the ground. "You earned that one."

"You okay, lass?" Patrick and Marge wore matching concerned looks. At Trish's nod, the old trainer took the reins and led Gatesby through the gate into the winner's circle.

"Fine job, Trish." John Anderson reached up to shake Trish's hand. At the same moment, Gatesby reached over and, before even Patrick realized what was happening, nipped his owner's shoulder. The camera caught the gelding's "who, me?" expression for all time.

"You—you . . ." Anderson sputtered, rubbing his shoulder and trying to shake hands with well-wishers at the same time.

Trish looked over at David, tried to catch her giggle, and failed miserably. She vaulted to the ground and hid her grin while unsaddling.

"Go ahead, all of you, laugh and get it over with." Anderson's blue eyes danced along with theirs. "If that's what I pay for a winner, I'll do it gladly. But Patrick, isn't there some way you can break him of it?"

"Did he really hurt you?" Trish stepped back off the scales and turned to the others.

"No, mostly jacket." Anderson shook his head. "It's just the principle of the thing."

Trish looked across the track to where David led the bay back to the barn. "I never knew he could run like that. I think the bump made him mad."

"Well, don't make a habit of it. I don't think my heart can stand it." Anderson turned to shake hands with someone else before saying, "Thanks, Trish. You did one fine job there."

"Welcome."

"Thank God you're all right," Marge muttered only for Trish's ears. "I'll meet you after you're dressed again. We're invited out for dinner."

"Okay. Yeah, I'm coming." She waved again at the group of students and let herself be captured by the waiting reporters.

———

By the time she'd showered and dressed, the crowd had gone home and only jockeys and clean-up crews called their good-nights in the cavernous building. Trish shivered as sound echoed. Such a short time ago she'd heard gun shots in this same hall. She walked out of the tunnel and crossed the infield to the backside.

Dusk softened the angles and muted the sounds of the track. Off in the distance a train rumbled by, its whistle warning drivers to beware. The sound echoed lonely in the letdown of the day.

Trish felt as if someone had pulled her plug and all her energy gurgled out like bath water down the drain. From watching where her feet stepped, she lifted her gaze to Mount Hood, off to the east. Setting sun brushed the tip of it pink and painted mauve shadows down the mountain's flanks.

A horse whinnied. Two others answered.

"Thank you, Father." She ordered her feet to move again.

When she rounded the corner to the Runnin' On Farm stalls, an excited chorus greeted her. A group of Prairie students had remained behind to congratulate her.

"That was some ride." Doug Ramstead picked her up in a bear hug and swung her around. He planted a kiss on her cheek before setting her back down.

Trish felt instant heat stain her neck and face. She glanced over to see David and Brad with duplicate eyebrows asking questions.

"Th-thanks." When she tried to step back, Doug kept one arm around her waist.

"Isn't she something?" Doug asked to no one in particular. "Man, I'd rather be sacked on a football field any day of the week than have some horse run into me."

Trish answered questions and teased her friends back. "Thanks for coming, guys. You all made this day really cool for me."

When they turned to leave, Doug dropped another kiss on her cheek. "See ya Monday, Tee." He strode off with the others, leaving Trish looking after him, shaking her head.

"See, I told you he likes you," Rhonda Seaboldt whispered after calling a last goodbye to their friends.

Trish glanced up at her redheaded best friend in all the world. "Gimme a break. He treats all the girls like that."

"Oh, really?" Rhonda must have practiced eyebrow raising along with Brad and David.

"Rhonda, see that bucket of ice-cold water over there?" Trish pointed to a black rubber bucket by the stall. "How'd you like to wear it?" She heard two identical snickers behind her. "Or you guys either."

Trish sank down in a canvas chair in the tackroom office. "Patrick, make them quit picking on me." She got to her feet again and opened the refrigerator door. "We got any Diet Coke in here or did those clowns drink it all?" She turned, popping the top on a soda can at the same time. "I'm starved. When do we eat?"

"Dinner's at the Red Lion." David leaned against the door frame. "Mom's already gone on with Bob Diego. We said we'd come as soon as we could. You ready?"

Trish caught herself in a mighty yawn. "I'd rather stop for pizza and go on home."

"Tough, kid." Tall, lean Brad Williams put an arm around her shoulders and guided her outside. "The price celebrities pay."

Trish punched him in the ribs with her elbow. "Knock it off or I'll sic Gatesby on you."

"Just so it isn't Doug the mighty Ramstead." Brad sidestepped her second punch.

Together the four Musketeers—as Marge had called them for years—and Patrick strode out to the parking lot.

————

Trish could hear the Thoroughbred Association board members and the others in the ballroom before walking through the doorway. But if she'd hoped to sneak in unnoticed, she'd hoped in vain. Bob Diego whistled for silence as soon as he saw her. Everyone broke into applause when they turned at his bidding.

Instant sunburn—so hot the heat would scorch her fingers if she touched her face. Trish wisely kept her hands out to shake those of the people around her. By the time they made it to the front of the room, she must have said "thank you" a hundred times.

"And now that we're all here, take your places and let's eat."

Trish looked longingly at the round table where her family settled into their seats. Instead she took the place Diego indicated at the head table by his side. What in the world was she doing up there? When she looked over at her mother, Marge just smiled back and sketched a nod.

David shrugged. Patrick raised his eyebrows and shook his head. Rhonda winked and blew her a kiss.

Trish rolled her eyes and concentrated on the salad in front of her. The question of why she was where she was hovered in the back of her mind through the prime rib and into the cheesecake.

"Can I get you anything else?" Diego asked. When Trish shook her head, he rose to his feet and clanked a knife against a water glass to call the group to attention.

When the hubbub quieted, he began. "This has been a momentous day for Portland Meadows and for all of us. I'm reminded of a verse I once heard: 'And a little child shall lead them.' Now I'm not calling this young lady by my side a child, but when the rest of us were wringing our hands and being taken in by a master con artist, she and her friends went out and did something to change the situation."

Applause broke out and gained momentum. A burning face seemed to be the order of the night. At his request, Trish rose to her feet.

"We have here, Trish, a check made out to your school, Prairie High, in appreciation for what all the students there did for us. Would you be willing to give our gift to them for us?"

Trish automatically took the envelope and shook his hand. "I—I . . ." She cleared her throat and started again. "Thank you, I had no idea . . ."

"We can't begin to thank you all, but maybe this will help." Bob started the applause and everyone joined him. People pushed back their chairs and stood, their clapping hands drowning out even the thundering of her heart.

Trish felt a tap on her shoulder. She turned. A waiter handed her another envelope and left. Trish looked up at Diego, who stared back with a shake of his head.

"I'll gladly take this money to Prairie on Monday morning, and thanks again." Trish waved one more time at a whistle from the back of the room and stepped away from the podium. After a sip of water while Bob added his closing remarks, she dug under the envelope flap and slit it open. When she opened the square sheet of paper, cut-out block letters seemed to leap off the page. "I'LL GET YOU."

CHAPTER TWO

Feeling gut punched was becoming a habit.

"Trish, what is it?" Robert Diego grabbed her arm when he felt her sway.

Trish handed him the sheet of paper. Her hand was shaking so violently she dropped it. Instead of reaching for the floating paper, she watched it flutter to the floor at her feet.

Diego knelt to pick it up. When he stood, the thundercloud furrowing his brow told Trish he'd read it. It didn't take long. The words were simple. "I'll get you."

Who, why? The words pounded through Trish's mind like horses going for the finish line. *I thought this was all over!* Trish gripped the back of her chair. Like fireworks exploding in the night, pure fury erupted from somewhere inside her. It steeled her knees and straightened her spine.

No one was going to make her live in fear again!

Jaw tight, Trish looked across the space to the table where her family waited. Marge half rose from the chair but sank down again at Trish's minuscule shake of the head.

"It seems we have a bit of a damper on our festivities." Bob Diego took the mike again. He shifted his gaze to Trish's face, as if asking permission to continue.

She nodded.

"If any of you know about this note or where it might have come from, we'd appreciate your sharing that information." He waved the paper in front of him. "Someone still seems to have it in for Trish. This one says 'I'll get you.' I think it's up to all of us to help any way we can in the investigation."

Trish moved closer to the podium. When Diego paused, she reached for the black mike. The steel in her spine had worked its way clear to her fingertips, and steel never trembles.

"As my dad would say, 'We're just giving God another chance to prove His power.' Whoever wrote this— this . . ." She snorted and shook her head. "He's sick, that's all. And evil. I think we all need to pray for God's protection—for me, for us, and for racing at Portland Meadows—so that we can have a clean sport." She could feel her words gaining strength. "And now we'll let the police deal with this. I don't know about you, but I have work to do in the morning. Thanks."

A nervous chuckle flitted around the room, then changed to applause. But when Trish looked at her mother, Marge wasn't clapping. Her hands were clenched together on the tabletop. Her bottom lip clamped between her teeth. Trish recognized the I-will-not-cry expression.

The group had just broken up, with many coming up to wish Trish the best, when Officer Parks strode in the door. The waiter trotted along beside him.

"I'm sorry, miss," the white-shirted man said. "If I'da

known what it was, I would never have given it to you."

"Who gave the envelope to you?" Parks removed his notebook while asking the question.

"One of the girls from the front desk. She just said there was a message for Trish Evanston. We do things like this all the time."

"I understand. Do you know the girl's name who gave you the envelope?"

The waiter smoothed a hand over his balding head. "Not really. I only work here for banquets, parttime, you know. I don't know very many of the regular staff."

"We'll take care of that later." Parks turned to Trish. "Sorry to meet again like this. I thought we had this problem solved."

Trish raised her eyebrows. "So did I." She could feel her mother standing at her side. "I'm afraid we left fingerprints on the paper."

"Yeah, well, we know yours by now."

"I'll bet that makes my mother real happy." Trish couldn't believe she'd said that. Here she was making a joke when she'd just gotten another threatening letter.

Officer Parks chuckled obligingly. The approval that beamed from his eyes congratulated Trish on handling the situation.

She hoped with grace. She felt her mother's hand resting on her shoulder. They'd been through a shooting together—surely they could handle a measly letter.

She could feel David fuming on her other side. He kept clenching and unclenching his fists. "I could kill him . . ." she heard him mutter under his breath.

She shot him a look meant to caution him, but the fire in his eyes never dimmed.

After all the questions had been asked, most of which

had no really helpful answers, they all walked out to the van together. Officer Parks pulled his squad car over, insisting on escorting them all home.

"What a day." Rhonda sighed, then yawned.

"Been enough excitement for you?" Brad opened the van door for them.

"I think so, even for me." Rhonda climbed into the backseat. "You okay, David?"

Without answering, David spun gravel turning onto the frontage road for Janzen Beach Shopping Center. He let up on the accelerator at a look from his mother, but even though he leaned back, his shoulder propped against the window, he drove straight-armed, not with his usual relaxed ease.

Stumbling at first, the conversation again picked up and eddied around the driver, who continued to ignore even direct questions.

"You going to give that check to Mr. Patterson on Monday or what?"

"Guess so. That was pretty neat, them voting money for Prairie." Trish glared at the back of her brother's head. "Don't you think so, big bro?" She looked at Rhonda and shook her head over her brother's obstinacy. "David, for Pete's sake, it's not as if he shot at me or something."

"Let him alone, Tee." The tone of Marge's voice brooked no argument.

Trish looked over her shoulder at Rhonda and Brad. They shrugged along with her.

Patrick sat rubbing his chin with work-worn fingers. "Give him some time, lass," he murmured for her ears alone. "He wasn't here for the last ones."

Trish sighed. Patrick was right. While she'd felt fury

burn through her at first, the flames had died away until only ashes remained. She couldn't—wouldn't stay mad like that. She'd have to let God take care of this again. He had before.

"That cute reporter, Curt Donovan, was taking notes like crazy," Rhonda said around a huge yawn, obviously changing the subject.

"Rhonda Louise Seaboldt . . ." Trish whipped around to shut her up but threw up her hands instead.

"Well, he is, and if I had a guy cute as that looking at me like he looks at you . . ."

Trish groaned. "Can't you think of anything besides guys?"

"Sure I can, you dope, but I think David almost smiled."

The words hissed in Trish's ear quite effectively set Trish to sputtering. "Say good-night, Rhonda."

"Good-night, all. See you in church tomorrow, or is it today?"

When they finally drove into Runnin' On Farm after dropping Brad off too, the area in front of the house looked like a parking lot—a full parking lot.

"What is going on?" Marge leaned back against the seat.

"Oh, no, reporters. See? That's the channel three van." Trish pointed at a white minivan with a big orange three on the side. "How'd they hear about this already?"

"Curt?" David made the name sound like a curse.

"No, he wouldn't do this to us." But it didn't matter how they heard. Questions and microphones, along with camcorders and eye-blinding strobe lights, met them as they stepped from the van. Before Trish had a chance to answer, Officer Parks pushed his way to the front and took Trish and Marge by the arms.

"I need to talk with these people first," he said to the crowd. "So you can wait around or come back in the morning, which would be much more polite."

"Right," a sarcastic voice came from the crowd. A rumble of chuckles agreed. "Just doing our job," said another. At every "How do you feel?" and "What will you do?" Trish just shook her head. The temptation to yell, "How do you think I feel when I get threatening letters? Like inviting the jerk out for ice cream?"

Marge took one of her arms and Officer Parks the other. They pushed through the crowd till they reached the steps. Trish stopped and turned while Marge unlocked the door. "Look, I'm tired. This has been a pretty big day. I'm mad clear through that—that *jerk* is starting up again, or whoever is. And I don't know any more than that. So you might as well head home. Good-night." She obeyed the tugging on her arm and followed Marge, Officer Parks, and Patrick into the house.

They heard doors slamming and car engines revving almost immediately afterward.

"There go the vultures." Parks unbuttoned his coat and drew out his little black notebook. "Trish, you handled them very well. Guess I really don't have to run interference for you."

"Well, I'm glad you did." Marge hung up her coat. "We'd still be out there if you hadn't. Now, how about I make some coffee?"

"Just a minute, Mrs. Evanston, if you would. I have something to tell you."

Marge turned back and crossed her arms across her chest, as if afraid of what she was going to hear. Unconsciously, Trish did the same.

"I'm afraid it's bad news. Kendall Highstreet was released on bail this afternoon."

"The developer who wanted to get Portland Meadows real cheap?" David leaned forward, his teeth snapping together like a shot. "He's crooked as they come. Doesn't attempted murder count for more than a few weeks in jail?"

"It will when he comes to trial, but for right now, the judge agreed to bail."

Trish felt the embers leap to life. So much for letting God handle all this.

"Now, I need all of you to go over this evening again—try to think of anything you might have missed. How could an outsider have known where you would be meeting? How about if you make that coffee and we'll all sit down and rehash this?"

Marge nodded. "Hot chocolate anyone? I can make that too."

This time it was Trish's turn to nod. When she started to follow her mother, Officer Parks shook his head. "I need to talk to you first."

While Marge served the hot drinks, they went over every detail together. But try as they might, nothing new came up. All anyone needed to do to learn about the dinner was to stand near some of the owners and eavesdrop.

"Plenty of people were talkin' about it." Patrick set his cup back on the coffee table. "Both by the track and at the barns. I heard 'em meself."

They all looked up when car lights flashed through the big square-paned living room window.

"That's probably Officer Jones now." Parks closed his notebook. "I requested protection for you, Trish. I—af-

ter the last scene, well, I don't think we can be too careful. She'll be here through the night, most likely turn
into your shadow." He turned to look at Marge. "Would
it be okay if she slept here on your sofa?"

"I—I guess so." Marge stood to answer the doorbell.

Trish glanced at David sitting in her father's recliner.
The light from the lamp glinted on dark curls that had
repeatedly been tangled by David's fingers. The set of his
jaw said it all. "She can have my bed. I'll take the sofa."

"But, David . . ." Trish didn't get any further. The look
he sent her could have sizzled a steak.

CHAPTER THREE

She's a cop? Trish blinked a second time.

Long blond hair, blue eyes fringed with impossibly long lashes, a cheerleader's smile, Officer Jones would fit in any high school in America. "Hi, my name's Amy, like short for Amanda." She looked like a Barbie doll next to Officer Parks.

Trish looked over at her brother. He had the sad appearance of a knocked-down bowling pin. The force of impact had slammed his chin to his chest.

"I'm Trish and this . . ." She swallowed a chuckle. "This is my big brother, David." She waited for him to respond, blink, answer something. "David?" Trish glanced at her mother in time to catch an infinitesimal shrug.

"I'm Marge Evanston and this is our trainer, Patrick O'Hern."

Trish watched David out of the corner of her eye. He sure got over mad quick. Now instead of the open-hanging-mouth look, he wore the famous Evanston smile, guaranteed to win votes. Or break hearts, as Rhonda had so often told him.

Amy smiled back at him, or rather up at him when he rose to his feet. "I hear you're going to Tucson this year. I have a brother who got his degree at the University of Arizona last year. How do you like it there?"

"F-fine." David swallowed, his Adam's apple dipping below the collar of his shirt.

Trish hugged her arms across her chest. If only Rhonda were here to see this.

"Think I'll be going now . . . let you all get acquainted." Parks brought Trish back to the real issue at hand. Amy wasn't just a friend dropping by. She was a police officer, here to guard Trish from some jerk who hated her.

Trish felt the shudders start at her feet and work their way up. Why? Who? *Why?* She stood and crossed the room, her legs feeling stiff, as if she'd locked her knees to keep upright.

"Now, if you think of anything else, you call me." Parks looked from Trish to her mother. "And Trish, go on about your daily life as normally as possible. Let Amy do the worrying for you. That's what we pay her for."

"Right. You'll let me know if you learn anything new, won't you?"

"Much as I can. Good-night now."

"I'll be goin' too. See you in the morning." Patrick followed the tall police officer out the door.

Marge closed the door behind them and leaned her forehead against the wooden frame for only a moment before turning and beginning to gather the coffee things together.

"Where's David?" Trish asked, setting the mugs on the tray.

"He said something about getting his sleeping bag. I

have my things with me. I don't want to put any of you out." Amy might look like a teenager and sound like one when she wanted to, but the tone now was all adult. "I'm not here as a guest."

Marge nodded, a polite smile barely lifting the corners of her mouth. "Let him fuss a bit. It'll take his mind off all this."

The two shared a woman-to-woman look that Trish recognized only because she and Rhonda used the same frequency. What fun the two of them could have over David being star struck by Amy! If only she weren't here for such a serious reason.

Trish sighed. She ran the tip of her tongue over her bottom lip. Oh, great . . . a cold sore popping out. She could feel the tender spot. By tomorrow it would probably cover half her lip. She headed for the bathroom to put salve on it.

The face in the mirror looked as if it had seen a ghost. She smeared on the cream and waited for the bite of it to penetrate her skin. In the meantime she smoothed skin cleanser over her eyes and face. The water running to get warm drowned out any sounds from the living room. In here it was easy to pretend this was an ordinary night. Racing during the day. Out for dinner. Company afterward. They'd done this plenty of times. She splashed her face with hot water, then cold.

But they hadn't had a police officer sleeping down the hall before. Would normal, whatever that was, ever return?

Trish followed the sounds of activity down the hall to David's room. The shock stopped her in the doorway. David was changing the sheets on his bed. Trish stifled the grin that threatened to crack her face and strolled over to the bed to help tuck in the blanket ends.

"Don't say a word." David flipped the navy bedspread in place and tossed her a pillow along with its case. "Just put that on while I dump the rest of this in the laundry."

"Yes, sir." Trish did as asked and folded the spread over the wrinkle-free pillow. *So David isn't immune to a pretty face after all.* She shook her head at her thoughts. He'd talked about a girl at WSU last fall, but that seemed three lifetimes ago. And who knew if he was seeing anyone in Tucson?

He returned with a set of matching towels and laid them across the foot of his bed. "Thanks, twerp." He dug his sleeping bag off the shelf of his closet and turned to leave. "You coming or what?"

The tip of her tongue found the blossoming cold sore again, but this time instead of feeling as if some unknown something was picking on her, she giggled when she followed him down the hall. David could get flustered too; the red on the back of his neck told her so.

"Don't even say a word." She caught his muttered command just before they entered the living room.

Keeping quiet was hard. Thoughts of all the times he'd hassled her about Red fed the desire to get even. But she managed. The conversation between the four of them seemed easy, as if Amy had been a guest before, or a friend they hadn't seen for a long time.

"Trish, if you hear or sense anything out of the ordinary, you tell me—immediately, okay?" Amy told her when they finally turned off the lights and headed down the hallway.

"I will." Trish stopped at David's door and pointed to the softly lit room. "You'll sleep here. My room is right across the hall. I need to be at the track to work horses at five, so it'll be a short night."

"Just wake me when you get up. What's your schedule for the rest of the day?"

"To church, back to the track, home again and homework." Trish paused a moment. "Oh yeah, and sometime in there we take David back to the airport."

"If I can get you anything, please tell me." Marge joined her daughter in the doorway. "I—I'm—we're grateful you're here."

"Thanks, Mrs. Evanston . . ."

"Marge."

"Okay, Marge. I'll try to stay out of your way as much as possible."

"Good-night then. Oh, and remember, we have an early-warning system in place already here."

"The collie?"

"His name is Caesar and he barks at anything unusual. Good-night then." Marge started to shut the door behind her as she left.

"Please leave that open so I can hear easily."

"Oh, I didn't think." Marge pushed the door open again.

Trish shivered at Amy's quiet command. As long as they were all talking, any danger seemed to fade away. Surely no one would bother her here at home. The guy wasn't that crazy, was he? She hung up her clothes when she took them off and slipped into her Mickey Mouse nightshirt. All the while her body accomplished her nightly ritual, her mind followed the twists and turns of trying to unravel this latest attack.

By the time she crawled under the covers, shudders racked her body from hair to toe. She reached up to turn off the lamp but pulled her arm back under the covers. Maybe she'd revert to her little kid days and sleep with the light on.

"Trish, you sleeping yet?"

"Sure, Mom, can't you tell?"

Marge entered the circle of lamplight and sat down on the edge of Trish's bed. "How are you *really* feeling?"

"Scared. Mad. Tired of it all."

Marge nodded. "Me too." She ran her fingers through the feathered sides of her graying hair. "I wish I could lock you up in a box so no one could get to you."

"Great. I've always wanted to live in a box." Trish rolled onto her back and laced her fingers behind her head. "I can't believe Highstreet is really so stupid."

"No one ever said criminals were smart."

"They shoulda just kept him in jail."

"That's one of the problems with our legal system— everyone has rights."

Trish glanced up to see a smidgen of a grin tugging at the corners of her mother's mouth. "I get to learn all about that in government, right?"

Marge nodded. "Back to the fear—you want to pray with me about that?"

Trish shook her head. While her own prayer life was improving, she still suffered when asked to pray with someone else, even her mother.

"You used to say your prayers with me."

Trish's gaze leaped from examining the cuticle on her left thumb to her mother's face. *Dad used to read my mind like that. Now can you?* She studied her mother's expression. "Is mind reading something all parents can do, or just you and Dad?"

Marge smiled gently and patted Trish's clasped

hands. "I'm praying for your safety and protection—God's promised special protection to widows and orphans."

"Thanks, but I'm not an orphan."

"Half a one . . . whatever. I claim all the love and protection I can." Marge paused; her gaze dropped to her hands before she looked back to Trish. "You need to pray for whoever is writing those notes. You can't let anger and bitterness come back into your heart."

Trish shook her head slowly from side to side. "I don't think so." But "pray for your enemies" leaped into her mind as she flatly denied her mother's wishes. And that wasn't even one of her memory verses. How did God do that?

She could feel the thoughts chasing each other around the corners of her mind. *Gotcha, didn't she?* Nagger seemed to chuckle.

Marge rose to her feet and bent down to give Trish a hug. "Think about it." She kissed her daughter's cheek. "And always remember that God loves you and so do I."

Trish wiped away the tears that sprang to her eyes at her mother's words. Her father had always said good-night the same way. She listened to the sounds her mother made getting ready for bed. Water running, the toilet flushing, the bed creaking—all audible because the bedroom doors were open. She reached up and shut off her light.

While the house quieted, other noises magnified: the scrape of a branch against her window, a dog, other than Caesar, barking somewhere, the shifting of a truck. Trish tried to swallow her stomach back down where it belonged. This was as bad as waiting for a stubborn horse to enter the starting gate for the third time.

She knew that sound was the tree outside; she'd heard it for years. Branch shadows ghost-danced on her wall, lit by the mercury light in the circular drive around. She scrunched her eyes shut, clamped her hands together, and tried to pray. When she pulled the covers over her head, all she could hear was her breathing—which grew more rapid until she flung the covers back, leaped from the bed, and stormed over to the window.

After checking the lock and drawing the lined drapes, she turned to a pitch-dark room. She could never remember drawing the drapes before. Within two strides, she slammed her little toe on the bed leg. Hopping on one foot so she could massage the two littlest toes on the other, she banged her knee on the footboard.

The sounds she muttered had no exact words, but if they had, they wouldn't have been the kind her mother liked to hear.

"Trish, are you all right?" Amy asked from the doorway. At least as far as Trish could tell, it was the general direction of the doorway. By now her eyes had adjusted to the darkness, so she reached for the lamp, knocking off the shade in the process.

Another mutter. "I'm fine. Just got banged up trying to close the drapes." She blinked against the light from the lamp.

"What's going on?" David loomed over Amy's back. "Trish?"

"Come on in, Mom. Everyone else is here." Trish rubbed her sore toes with one hand and combed back her hair with the other. "I was just closing the curtains to keep out the sounds and I banged into the bed. I'm not used to it being so dark in here."

"What did you hear?" Amy leaned her hip against Trish's desk.

"The tree scraping on the window, a car . . ." Trish listed the sounds. "Guess I'm just spooky tonight."

"Yeah, something like the rest of us." David imitated Trish's act of pushing hair back with his fingers. A dark curl dropped back over his forehead as if it belonged there.

Marge returned from looking out the window. "Your foot okay?"

"It will be. Sorry to cause such a hassle." Trish pushed her hair back again. By the time they all left, she felt like hiding her head under her pillow. Maybe if she'd done that in the first place, this sideshow wouldn't have happened.

After turning out the light again, she snuggled down under her covers. "God, this is crazy. I've never been scared here at home before, at least not like this. If you've got extra angels up there who need a job, could you just put 'em around the house?" Her mother's suggestion to pray for the developer slipped into her mind. The thought brought a blaze of anger instead. "How can he do such a thing? And if it isn't him, then who?" Her mind took off with a will of its own.

Trish jerked it back. "Please help me do my best tomorrow. Amen." She turned over and settled herself on her other side. *Three praises. I forgot the praises.*

When are you gonna learn? Nagger sounded like he was shaking his head.

"Thank you for the wins today, for the money for Prairie from the TBA, for having David home . . ." She rubbed the cold sore with her tongue. "For healing my lip in advance . . ." She felt herself smiling. "And for all my friends." She sighed at the memory of crimson and gold going crazy at the track. "Amen."

This time when she took a deep breath, she could feel the tension drain out of her body and leave a puddle of warmth behind. *Thank you again, Father.*

———————

By the time Trish had worked all of the racing string in the morning, she'd gotten over watching over her shoulder and checking to see if anyone she didn't know was hanging around. Amy seemed right at home. She and Patrick watched the works from the raised and covered viewing stand by the gate leading onto the track from the backside. He'd volunteered to explain things to her so she could have a better idea how to watch Trish.

At first Trish caught herself paying more attention to the pair, but by the second horse, she forgot about that too and just did her job. Besides, she was freezing. The rising sun had faded the eastern sky to gray with a thin stripe of gold between the overcast and the horizon. But the breeze making fog tendrils dance blew right through her, making even her bones shiver.

"You've turned into a California girl for sure," David teased when Trish wiped her dripping nose on a tissue pulled from a box in the office.

"Yeah, you get out there where the wind hits you and we'll see who's used to warmer weather." She tucked her gloved hands under her armpits and stamped her feet. "I'm going to buy some of those socks with warmers in them and dig out my long johns."

"Well, you've only one after this, and I promise to turn the heater in the truck up full blast." He boosted her into the saddle of the gelding Patrick was training for another owner. "I'm not sure what Patrick wants done here, so you better ask him. You gonna ride the mounts you have for this afternoon?"

Trish shook her head. "Not and make it to church." She checked her watch. "We better hurry." She tapped her brother on top of the head with her whip. "You want me to say anything to Amy for you?"

"Get outa here."

Trish sniffed again. If only her nose would quit dripping. She felt the hackles rise on the back of her neck. Who was that man walking down the aisle to Diego's barns? "This has got to stop!" At the tone of her voice, the gelding jigged to the side.

Trish patted the horse's neck and crooned an apology to the high-stepping animal. "Not your fault, fella. You just do what you know is right. We'll go around nice and easy to loosen you up, then a breeze for the clockers." Trish raised her hand to Patrick and shivered again as the wind hit her. "Maybe we should all move to California."

Brad arrived just when Trish brought the gelding back to the barn. "Sorry I'm late. My alarm didn't go off." He stopped and shot Trish a questioning look when he saw Patrick and Amy walking back to the stalls.

"That's Amy Jones," Trish said after vaulting to the ground. "Because of the note last night, Parks brought me a guard."

"Well, she could guard me any day."

"You and David. She's really a nice person."

"I bet."

"Brad Williamson, you're as bad as your friend over there. Now, I gotta get home and get warmed up. How about you finish grooming this guy?"

When Amy and Patrick joined them, Brad nudged Trish until she relented and introduced him. Had everyone gone girl or boy crazy but her?

"I don't know about you guys, but I need to get something to eat and get ready for church. David, you coming or what?"

Back at the truck, Trish swallowed a snort. David opened the door for them. Trish stepped back to let Amy sit in the middle and caught a nod of approval from her non-smiling brother.

"No, I'll take the window . . . lets me see better." Amy ushered Trish in first.

Trish shrugged when David shot her a glare as he started the engine. She adjusted the heater controls and soon a blast of hot air could be felt into her boots.

"I forgot how cold it can be out there."

"Yeah, well we froze in the fog at Bay Meadows, even if it was California."

"But it always burned off there. I think I'm beginning to like it down south." Trish rubbed her hands together.

"I've only been south twice. Once for my brother's graduation"—Amy pulled the cap off her head and let her blond hair swing down around her shoulders—"and once to Disneyland. My fiancé says maybe we'll go there on our honeymoon."

Trish could feel David deflate. Wait till she saw Brad again.

Cinnamon roll perfume met them at the door when they pulled off their boots at the jack and entered the dining room.

"Thought you could eat in shifts while taking turns for the shower." Marge set a plate of bacon on the table. "Amy, would you like coffee or hot chocolate?"

"Coffee, please."

Trish heard them visiting when she headed for the shower. She'd have to wear her hair in a braid today, no time to wash and dry it.

———

Everything was fine until Pastor Mort started the prayers after the sermon. Trish had no trouble with him praying for safety for her and the family, but when he began praying for the person causing the harassment, she wanted to plug her ears. He didn't say anything like "God, get the man" or "Help the police capture him."

Instead he said, "Father, bring this person to a knowledge of you and your will for his life that he may know your love and forgiveness."

Trish felt like gagging.

CHAPTER FOUR

When a flute began to play the opening bars for her song, she breathed a sigh of relief. Right now she really needed those eagle's wings to lift her up and the hand of God to hold her. She shared her songbook with Amy and sang with all her heart.

"I love that song," Amy said after the service was over.

"Me too. It's kinda become my theme song. When I'm really down, it helps pick me up."

"I can see why."

"Come on, David, I need to get back to the track," Trish muttered. But getting out of church quickly might take one of God's miracles. By the time her mother had introduced Amy to a dozen people and others had extended their assurance of praying for the family, time had sprouted wings.

"Can I help?" Rhonda whispered from right behind Trish's shoulder.

"You could yell fire!"

"Nope, I thought more along the lines of sneaking you out the back, but then your bodyguard might think you'd been snatched."

"Rhonda, you've been watching too many movies. Amy is *not* my bodyguard."

"She's not your long-lost cousin either. Wish I hadn't let you take me home first last night. I missed out on all the excitement."

"Right. You can have all this excitement. I need to get to the track and soon. My first mount is in the second race."

Trish smiled when someone else said something to her, but she could feel her mask beginning to crack.

Amy caught Trish's look and nodded. Suddenly they were outside the church and on their way to the car.

"Hey, you're good," Trish and Rhonda said at the same time.

Amy grinned at them. "You should have said something sooner. One of the first things we learned at the Academy was crowd control."

"And you never offended anyone." Trish shook her head. "I should have you teach me some tricks."

"Sure 'nough." Amy climbed into the backseat of the van last and smiled at David when he slammed the door.

Trish watched Amy watch the surrounding area. While carrying on a conversation, Amy still scoped out the parking lot, the cars, and the people getting into them. If this was one of God's answers to prayer, Trish decided, it was one of those easy to be thankful for.

By the time Trish arrived at the track, she had to head directly to the jockey room.

"Will my being there cause a problem for you?" Amy asked halfway across the infield. "I could wait outside, kind of mingle with the crowd."

"No, you're short enough that you could be a visiting jockey."

"Great! What I know about riding could fit on the point of a pencil. Just say I'm your cousin visiting—like we have been. The less lies we tell, the less chance there is of getting messed up. Now, have you noticed anyone unusual?"

Trish grinned at her companion. "Look around you. Is there anyone here *not* unusual?"

Just then one of the bug boys walked by and grinned. "Buenas dias." He wore fringed leather chaps and a purple helmet, and sported a handlebar mustache under a nose that looked as if it had met one too many fists.

Amy returned the smile. "I mean anyone you don't know. There is definitely a collection of characters here."

"Yeah, this is really my extended family. Dad started bringing me here when I was about ten. I always wanted to race."

"And now you're doing it. You're lucky."

A few early fans leaned on the rails; others studied their racing programs. When Trish looked up to the glass-fronted stands, reflecting the gray clouds, she felt a chill snake up her spine. Someone could be watching her and she wouldn't even know it. She responded to a "Hi, Trish" and a "Good luck, little lady," but the arm at her elbow didn't allow for stopping to visit. For the first time, Trish felt stomach-relaxing relief at the thought of her escort.

The other jockeys greeted Amy when Trish introduced her, and then continued their business of preparing for the upcoming races.

As Trish went about her routine, she nearly forgot Amy was there; the woman blended into the woodwork, almost. Trish polished her boots and applied wax to all five pairs of her goggles, stacking them on the front of her helmet and snapping them in place. She'd use one till it was dirty, then bring down the next pair. The muddier the track, the more goggles used per race.

After the first race had been called, Trish moved to the floor for her stretches. Extenders, twists, straddles, all used different muscles and stretched joints. The more limber she was the less chance of injury. Her father had drilled her well.

She'd just pulled a white long-sleeved turtleneck over her head when Genie Stokes returned from running in the first race.

"How'd you do?" Trish asked, popping her head out of the shirt like its namesake.

"Don't ask." Genie sank down on the bench beside Amy. "That filly acted like she'd never seen a racetrack before, let alone the starting gate." She shook her head. "And I know she has because I've been riding her for training."

Trish finished lacing her white pants and sat down to pull on her boots. "Well, starting tomorrow, Patrick wants you to ride for us in the morning."

"I know. Maybe he'll teach me more about handling youngsters like that one."

"Was it her first race—a maiden, right?" Amy asked.

"It was her first, but maiden means any horse that hasn't won a race yet, not just their first." Genie stepped to the mirror and wiped a smear of dirt off her cheek.

"Oh. And here I thought I was being pretty smart."

"Well, if you're around us for any length of time, you'll learn plenty. Most of us don't know anything but horse talk."

The squawk box announced riders for the second

race to the scales, so Amy and Trish followed another jockey out the door. *Much as I like you,* Trish thought, *I hope you're not my shadow long enough to learn all about racing.*

"Sure wish I could keep you home away from all these crowds," Amy muttered when they joined the parade of jockeys out to the spoke-wheel-shaped saddling paddock. Spectators lined the rails, some leaning over with programs to be autographed. Others hollered their greetings and encouragement.

To Trish, the scene felt familiar and comfortable—a far cry from San Mateo, where, as a loser, she'd had few fans. Maybe being a big frog in a little pond wasn't such a bad thing after all.

She blocked out thoughts of everything but the coming race when she joined Bob Diego in stall three. "Bob, I'd like you to meet my cousin, Amy Jones, she's visiting here from Spokane."

"I'm glad to meet you."

Trish met his gaze without flinching, hoping he'd pick up on what Amy's job really was. No one brought their cousin into the saddling paddock unless that "cousin" owned the horse.

Diego studied the petite blonde for a moment, before his gaze shifted back to Trish, crinkles tightening the corner of his dark eyes. "I'm *very* glad you brought Amy along, mi amiga. Family is so important, is it not?"

Trish nodded, grateful for his understanding. She stepped to the gelding's head and let him sniff her arm before rubbing his cheeks and up behind his ears. "How ya doin', fella? Long time no see." She had ridden him the year before, once into the winner's circle. "Think we can get in line for the camera again?"

"He should do well. He's in top condition and rarin' to go."

The call came for riders up, so Trish gave the dark bay one last pat and turned for a leg up. Diego checked the cinch again and looked up at Trish. "You've a big field, and with a mile to go, he'll need a kick left for the stretch. He likes being in the lead, but the last time he set too fast a pace and came in with a fourth."

"I'll watch him." Trish smoothed the black mane to the right and gave the gelding a final scratch when Diego backed the animal out of the stall. She nodded at the greeting from the pony rider and waved when someone called her name. How could she ever have thought about giving up racing? Her butterflies gave a leap just to remind her they still resided in her midsection, the crowd roared when the horses trotted onto the track, and the horse beneath her jigged a response to the excitement. Yeah, this was what she was born for.

When they cantered back past the grandstands, the starting gates were wheeled into position behind them. The roar of the crowd drowned out the tractor noise, but Trish concentrated only on the grunts of the animal beneath her as he tugged against the bit, wanting to catch up with the two ahead. As Diego had said, his horse was primed and ready.

When Trish looked ahead she could see the number one horse giving both the jockey and the pony rider a bad time. The gray gelding swung his rump to the side and jerked against the lead tie.

"Sure glad we're not next to him," she sang to her mount. "But let him use all his energy now. We have a race to win." Her horse snorted and tossed his head, as if in agreement.

Behind the gates, number one continued to act up. He refused to enter the stall, sitting back on his haunches when the handlers tried to lead him in. Trish trotted her mount around in a tight circle, keeping him active so he'd be ready. After the second refusal to the gate, number one struck out with his front feet.

Send him back to the barns, Trish felt like telling them. *We don't need trouble out here.* She could feel her horse begin to tense in response. "Easy, fella. His bad manners have nothing to do with you."

The gate assistants motioned the remaining horses into the stalls. One by one they entered and settled. This time number one walked in as if he'd never hesitated. The gates clanged shut. The pause.

Trish forgot about the gating problem, focusing all her attention on the horse she rode. She could feel him settle and gather his weight on his haunches.

The shot, the gates clanged open, and they were off.

The field remained bunched going into the first turn and then both the leaders and trailers emerged. Trish kept her mount running easily, one off from the leader and abreast with another. He didn't fight for the lead as Diego had warned, instead seeming content to let Trish do her job.

The three leaders held their position down the back-stretch and going into the far turn, but the pace was fast. Trish hung above her horse's withers, aware of a horse coming up on the outside but not ready to move yet. Going into the stretch, the lead horse slowed and the rider went to the whip.

Trish loosened the reins. "Okay, fella, now." The gelding spurted forward. With each step he left his running mate behind and gained on the front-runner. He stretched out again and flew past the leader as if he'd been shot from a cannon. Trish let him go, glorying in the speed and power beneath her. No one was coming even close behind them. When they drove across the finish line, her mount was still gaining speed.

"That was some race," Bob Diego greeted her back in front of the winner's circle. "You played him just right."

"I don't think he even needed a jockey. He knew what to do. I just went along for the ride."

"Well, it was certainly a good ride. Thank you, mi amiga. You can ride my horses anytime."

After posing for the pictures, Trish weighed in and headed for the jockey room. Amy picked her up at the fence and paced the dirt track with her.

"Was that as much fun to ride as it was to watch?"

"More. That old boy could have gone farther and faster if I'd let him. The long rest hasn't hurt him any."

"I might turn into a racing fan by the time this assignment is over." Amy held the gate for her. "You should hear all the good things the crowd says about you. Except of course for those rooting for another horse."

"Naturally." Having Amy shadowing her again brought back the fears Trish had managed to forget on her circles around the track.

Trish picked up her silks for the next race and entered the jockey room. Racing in two, three, and four didn't leave her much time to relax, but then she didn't have to worry about cooling off too much either.

The overcast deteriorated to mist by the time she trotted her next mount onto the track. Trish hunched her shoulders to keep warmer, wishing she'd switched to her warmer turtleneck. The newly risen wind tugged at neck and sleeves, sending the cold deep into her skin.

By the time all seven horses were in their gates, the mist had turned to drops. When Trish lowered her goggles into place, she felt grateful for the remaining pairs. Shame the glasses didn't have wipers.

The filly she rode broke clean and surged forward with her running mates. Down the backstretch they galloped, shifting positions when first one then another took the lead. Into the turn Trish and another ran stride for stride. Out of the turn the front-runner slowed, then surged again at the whip.

The other jockey went for the whip. Trish loosened the reins, but when her mount failed to respond, she smacked the filly with a right-handed stroke and then another.

But the spurt of speed wasn't enough. They came in with a show by only a nose.

"Sorry, girl. That was my fault." She stood in her stirrups to bring the filly back down. *You shoulda gone to the whip sooner,* she scolded herself. *Not all horses are voice-trained like yours are, and you know it.* After adding a couple of choice names to the roster, she apologized to the trainer as well.

The woman shook her head. "I thought you brought her in real well. That's the best she's ever done. You can ride for me anytime."

But the vote of confidence failed to override the berating Trish was still giving herself when Amy fell in with her. As Amy opened the gate, Trish felt the hairs on the back of her neck tingle. She stopped and looked around, seeking a strange face or something out of the ordinary, like Amy had told her to look for.

"What is it?" Amy had placed herself in front of Trish nearly before Trish stopped.

"I don't know. Maybe just the rain making my back chilled." Trish turned at the tug on her elbow and continued up the hall to the jockey room. "I didn't see or hear anything—just all of a sudden, I had the creeps."

"Glad to hear you have those senses. Makes my job easier." Amy hustled her from the silks room to the jockey room. "Next time, don't stop. You set yourself up as a target that way."

Trish felt as spooky as her horse for the next race. Rain falling steadily served to curb the audience excitement, and the snap and whoompf of an opening umbrella made her horse snort and leap to the side.

Her heart started pounding before the umbrella finished stretching. She ordered her hands to relax, loosening one finger at a time. The urge to look over her shoulder struck so powerfully she almost grabbed her chin to keep her concentration to the front.

You're nuts to react like this. She took up the inner scolding again. *Your job is to ride this horse, right now, to the best of your ability. Not look over your shoulder because you've got a bad case of the spooks.*

The horses entered their gates willingly as if they all understood that the faster they got this over with, the faster they could get out of the rain. The shot, the gates swung open, and Trish forgot all but the horse beneath her and those around her. In the number four slot, they broke in the middle of the pack. The eight animals bunched around the turn, and being right in the middle, Trish had no place to go. Not without bumping someone else.

She ignored the urge to scream her frustration at the heavens. Would someone get moving and get out of her way? But when the chance came, the filly took too long to move and the hole closed. Down the stretch when the horses strung out, Trish, even going to a steady whip, could move her no farther than fourth.

Start in the middle and end in the middle. If Trish had given herself a tongue-lashing before, it was only a practice run. Now she flayed herself with both anger and purpose. She'd done a terrible job with this horse. *All because you can't keep your mind on what you're doing! If you can't do better than this, stay home.*

Patrick just shook his head when she made that same statement back at the barns. "Ye know, lass, you can't blame yourself for everything. Those things just happen."

Trish shot him a look guaranteed to fry eggs.

David's comment earned an identical look.

"Trish thought she sensed something wrong back there," Amy said.

Trish felt like throttling her bodyguard.

David grabbed Trish's arm and brought her to a stop. "What did you see?"

"Nothing, big brother." Trish put all the sarcasm she could muster into her voice. "It was nothing at all."

"That's it, I'm staying home." David dropped her arm and headed back to the office. "Mom can cancel my flight."

"Yeah, right. As if you could protect me or something." Trish strode up the walk. "Let's just get home. I'm freezing."

By the time they crossed the I–5 bridge over the Columbia River, neither Trish nor David were speaking, especially not to each other.

"Have you any idea what gave you the feeling of being watched?" Amy finally broke the silence.

Trish shook her head. "I've tried to figure it out, but nothing. Maybe I'm just being paranoid or something."

"Gut feelings are pretty important. I'm just glad you're not racing for the next two days. Maybe we'll have a breakthrough by then and you won't have to worry anymore."

"I wish." The shiver that shimmied up Trish's back had nothing to do with the dampness of the day.

"But, Mom, you've always said an extra pair of eyes or hands or whatever makes for light work. In this case, the more of us to watch out for Trish the better. If I miss a few classes, it's no big deal."

"It *is* a big deal, but you don't have to worry about it, because you'll be there." Marge planted her hands on her hips and the set of her chin warned everyone not to argue with her.

"Mother, be reasonable. You and Trish could be in real danger—at least Trish is. They keyed her car and shot at her, remember?"

"Oh, I remember all right. I was there. But you can't guard your sister and neither can I. Amy is doing her best, and the rest we have to trust to God."

"He didn't seem to do so well last time," David muttered under his breath.

Trish leaned her hips against the counter, sipping a cup of hot chocolate. One eyebrow raised at David's comment. But she kept her mouth shut—with difficulty. *Let them battle it out for a change,* she thought. *They don't pay much attention to what I say anyway.*

Amy entered the kitchen and joined Trish against the counter. "Would you like the latest bulletin?" she asked when a silence lasted more than a second or two. When the two turned to face her, she included Trish in her smile.

"Parks says Highstreet has a solid alibi, so that, at least temporarily, leaves him out of the picture. He wondered if there was anyone you might have offended at the track, Trish, that could do a copycat crime? Since this was so well publicized, thanks to our esteemed press corps, things like that happen more than you know."

Trish looked to both Marge and David and then shook her head. "I've been gone so much, and then helping to solve the problem out at the track, that I've hardly even seen anyone, let alone ticked them off."

"Could anyone be jealous?"

"Course, she won the Triple Crown, didn't she?" David crossed both his arms over his chest and his ankles as he leaned back against the counter. "And she drives a flashy red convertible, travels around the country, gets her name in all the papers, has the money to buy what she wants. I'm sure there's no one the least bit jealous."

"David."

"Gets shot at, becomes a heroine . . ."

"We know all those things, David." Amy's quiet voice stopped his tirade like his mother's hadn't been able.

"Then why don't you do something about it?"

"We are."

"They are." Marge added.

"I'll get it." Trish pushed herself upright and crossed to the ringing phone. "Runnin' On Farm. Trish speaking."

"I can tell."

"Who is this?"

"Don't you wish you knew."

CHAPTER FIVE

Trish's hand shook so hard she dropped the phone.

"Dial tone," Amy said after grabbing the receiver. "What did he say?"

"I—I didn't hear all of it." Trish wrapped her arms around her middle to keep from shattering into small pieces. "To—to watch out."

David slammed his hand down on the counter. "And you think I'm leaving here? No way!"

"Okay, let's all calm down." Amy raised her hands for silence. "From now on, Trish, you don't answer the phone. I will. We'll put a tap on it so maybe we can get him that way. David, I know you mean well and I appreciate what you're trying to do. But right now, we're going to try to go on with life as usual. Please, let your mother take you to your plane as you planned."

"The best thing you can do is pray for all of us." Marge placed her hands on her son's shoulders and stared deep into his eyes.

"Doesn't seem to do much good. Look at all that has happened."

"But, David, no one's been hurt."

"What about Trish's car?"

"As I said, no one's been hurt. God is doing His job; now let's all of us do ours."

"And mine is going back to school." David sighed and shook his head. "This is against my better judgment."

"I know. And I appreciate that."

Trish watched the interchange between the two people she loved most on this earth and marveled at the way they understood each other. *Dad and I were like that,* she thought. *I miss that. Dad, I miss you. What would you do with all this stuff that is going on?*

David gathered his things as his mother requested and brought his bags to the door. "You be careful, Tee. Whoever this guy is, you can't count on him to make sense."

"I know and you take care of yourself." Trish fought back the burning behind her eyes and wrapped both arms around her brother. "I miss you when you're gone. Now that you've been home again, I figured out how much."

"I'll see you in Kentucky in less than two weeks, then it'll be Christmas before you know it."

"Thanks. With all I have to do, that doesn't sound too comforting."

As soon as Marge and David left, Amy got on the phone to order a tap and bring Parks up-to-date on the latest development.

Trish wandered back to her bedroom to change clothes and head for the barn. She whistled for Caesar and pounded down the cedar deck stairs fully expecting the collie to bound into view. She whistled again. No yipping, cavorting bundle of energy danced around her legs and tried to lick her nose.

Fear niggled at her mind.

Must be a female in heat somewhere around here. She forced herself to think of reasons for his absence. *Or he's off chasing rabbits or . . .* She couldn't keep the thoughts going. Caesar *never* left the farm when they weren't home. He took his guard-dog duties as seriously as did the Secret Service around the President.

Trish whistled again. "Caesar! Hey fella, Caesar."

The horses whinnied from down in the paddocks. A crow cawed from up in a fir tree. But no sable collie with a snowy white ruff whimpered an apology for being late.

Trish debated. Should she tell Amy that Caesar was missing? Or should she just get the chores done so she could go look for him? *God, help me.* She shot her arrow prayer heavenward and trotted down to the barns. To-night she would put all the horses in their stalls and feed them there.

"You guys seen Caesar?" she asked the nickering ba-bies. Miss Tee and Double Diamond greeted her with tossing heads and quivering nostrils. They lipped their carrots and nuzzled her shoulder as if she were a long-lost friend. "Don't care for the yucky weather, huh?" Trish snapped the lead shanks onto their halters and trotted the young horses up to the barn.

Where was Caesar? Fear dried her mouth so her whistles lost their soar.

Old gray Dan'l, the gelding who'd helped train her in the fine arts of thoroughbred racing, whinnied repeat-edly, as if afraid she might forget him. Trish trotted back down the lane and stopped at his paddock. "Hey, easy on the fence." She pushed him back while hugging his gray neck at the same time. "Come on, let's get you up to the barn. You seen Caesar?"

Dan'l munched his carrot without answering her.

By the time she'd fed everybody, dusk faded into darkness. The drifting mist caught rainbows in the area lit by the mercury yard lamp. She trotted up the front walk and entered through the front door.

Amy was still on the phone.

"Caesar's missing." Trish grabbed the truck keys off the pegboard by the phone and headed for the door again.

"Hang on, Trish. I'll come with you." Amy finished her conversation and hung up. "Is this unusual?"

"He never leaves, especially when we're not home." Trish waited by the door for Amy to get her coat.

Car lights from Patrick's new half-ton pickup met them back in the drive. He stopped at Trish's wave.

"Caesar's missing. Thought I'd check the road just in case." The thought of her beloved collie lying in a ditch made her want to heave.

"You looked through the barns?"

"Not really. Fed the horses though and everyone's in."

"I'll search down there."

Half an hour later, Trish turned the truck back into the lane at Runnin' On Farm. She'd call Rhonda and Brad to ask for their help too.

"This would be so much easier in the daylight." She banged her fist against the steering wheel. "Where could he be?"

"Wish I knew." Amy opened her door. "Wish I knew."

"No one would hurt a dog, would they?" Trish finally voiced the thought that had been flitting around in her head.

"I hope not."

The answer didn't sound convincing.

Trish spent the next half hour calling some of the neighbors to ask if they'd seen the dog. The phone rang and rang at Rhonda's. Brad answered on the second ring.

"Sure I'll help call," he said. "Want me to go out with you again?"

"Not right now. How about asking if anyone has a dog in heat? That's the only thing I can think of that would get him to leave."

"Sure will. Have you walked down by the creek and way out in the pastures?"

"Not really. He just never answered, so I figured he wasn't there."

"I'll be over after I make these calls. You got a good flashlight?"

Trish hung up and leaned against the counter, staring out into the night without really seeing it. Where could he be?

She walked over to the refrigerator and took out a Diet Coke. "You want something to drink or anything?" The guilties grabbed her. Some kind of hostess she was.

Amy looked up from the notes she was writing. "No thanks—and, Trish, you don't have to play the good hostess with me. I'm a member of the family, remember? I can help myself."

Trish nodded. Where could Caesar be? She sipped her drink and went to stand at the sliding glass door. When she flipped on the light switch, her mother's baskets of pink and purple fuschias sparkled with droplets of mist. Soon they would be put to sleep for the winter before the frost killed them.

Trish shuddered at the thought of being put to sleep. She slid open the door and stepped out on the deck, staying under the overhang of the house to keep dry.

Country silence filled the crisp, damp air. Listening hard, she caught the tinkle of runoff in the downspouts. A breeze sent droplets cascading from the fir trees and plopping on the ground.

Trish held her breath. What had she heard?

"Caesar?" She waited again. Had it been a whine?

She whistled, three tones pleading for an answer. She held her breath, concentrating everything she had on listening.

The sound came again, weak, distant, sad.

Trish flung open the door and grabbed the high-powered battery light from its nest plugged into the wall. "Amy, I think I heard something." Out the door, down the steps and around the deck, quartering the ground with the intensive beam, Trish searched each shadow and cranny.

Down on her hands and knees she flashed the light underneath the deck. "Caesar? That you, fella?"

A faint whimper seemed to come from the back corner.

"You hear that?" Trish asked as Amy crouched down beside her. The sound came again.

"Yes. Can we get under there?" Amy leaped to her feet. "I've got another flashlight in the car. And a tarp to pull him out on."

"Go tell Patrick. He might be able to help us."

As soon as Amy left, Trish concentrated again on the sounds from under the deck. A whimper came in response to her gentle, "Caesar? You under there? What's happened to you?"

She edged underneath, digging in with her elbows to pull herself forward. When she tried to use her knees, she bumped her butt on the cedar joist above her. "Ouch." She flashed the light again but still couldn't see her dog.

Laying her cheek flat on the cold, damp ground, she scanned the beam under the low-lying joists. One red eye reflected back at her. "Good dog, Caesar. I'm coming." Caesar huddled three joists over.

Trish back-crawled as fast as she could, paying no attention to bumps and muddy spots.

"You found him?" Amy met her as Trish stood upright again.

"Yes, he's back in the corner." Trish dropped to her knees again at the right joist. "There's no room for two to work under there. I'll go back with the tarp, roll him onto it, and then pull it out, I guess."

"We'll use this rope to help pull. You think he'll let you handle him?"

Trish paused for only a moment. "Of course. He's my dog."

"Ye found him then, lass?" Patrick joined them.

"Uh-huh. Pray for us, Patrick." Trish shoved the tarp under the wooden frame and crawled after it. "I'm coming, old man. Hang on."

"Here, I can help you from this side." Amy elbowed into the adjoining crawl space, pushing her light ahead of her, just like Trish. Matching grunts marked their progress as they dug in their elbows and pulled themselves forward. "Ugh, I hate spider webs."

The smell of wet earth filled Trish's nostrils and clogged her throat. Her jerking light reflected off the beams above her and glistened on the wet slime covering the bare ground. No eyes reflected back from the dog she knew lay ahead.

"Caesar, fella, you okay?"

Only the panting of her partner broke the stillness. "Can you see him?" Amy's voice seemed almost in her ear.

"Not yet. Never realized how big this deck really is."

"Or how hard belly crawling under this decking would be."

"There he is." Trish dug and pulled faster, almost crawling over the tarp in her eagerness. The muddy form ahead of her never moved. "Caesar?"

She swallowed the bite of fear stinging her throat and causing tears to blur her vision. "Caesar, please fella, hang in there. We're coming for you." She shoved the tarp next to him and inched across it to lay her hand over his ribs.

She clamped her teeth on her bottom lip. *God please.* His matted fur lay still. She pressed harder. There under her fingers a faint heartbeat. "He's alive—barely."

"Okay, can you see any blood?"

Trish flashed the light over the inert dog. "No. Just dirt, like he's crawled a long way."

With trembling fingers she spread the tarp, accepting the help Amy provided from under the cedar joist. "Ouch." She only acknowledged the bang on her head with the word while she slid her fingers under Caesar's shoulders.

"I've got his hindquarters. Now on three, we'll pull him onto the tarp." Amy reached as far as her shoulders. "This would be a good time to have basketball-player arms." She clenched the matted fur. "Okay—one, two, three."

Together they heaved. Trish banged her head against the cedar boards above her and ended up with her nose buried in Caesar's muddy shoulder. He didn't move. She scrunched backward. "Okay, you ready? We'll go again. One, two, three."

Caesar lay on his side on the tarp. Trish laid her face against his muzzle while she caught her breath. A warm tongue flicked the side of her cheek.

"He's alive. Come on, Patrick, pull." Trish scrambled backward as fast as her knees and elbows permitted, trying to keep ahead of the sliding tarp.

"I've got your flashlight." Once out Amy pushed herself into a kneeling position at the same moment as Trish. "How is he?"

"He can't lift his head but he licked my cheek. We call him the fastest tongue in the west." Trish grabbed the corners of the tarp. "Come on, let's get him to the truck."

"Marge has the van running. She already called the vet." Patrick hefted along with the two women and together they lugged the heavy body around the house and up to the open back doors of the van.

"Dr. Bradshaw will meet us at the office." Marge gave Trish a boost so she could follow the dog into the van. "Amy, you coming?"

"I'll ride back here with Trish." Amy clambered onto the carpet. Patrick slammed the doors at the same time Marge closed hers, and she immediately set the van in motion.

"Can you feel any broken bones or anything?" Amy joined Trish in probing the dog's legs and spine.

"No. This doesn't make sense. He was fine this morning, so unless he was hit on the road . . ."

Amy smoothed her fingers over the dog's grimacing lips, revealing teeth in pale gums. "See the way his head is pulled back?"

"Then what could it be?" Trish wiped her drippy nose on her sleeve. "Come on, fella, hang in there." She grabbed the carpeted wheel well for support as her mother swung around a corner.

"Trish, could he have eaten anything—anything that—"

"Like what? He got into a salmon years ago and nearly died from salmon poisoning—" Trish bit off her sentence. "Poisoning. Do you think he's been poisoned? Who would poison a dog like Caesar?"

"Could he have gotten into something for coyotes or some such?"

"No one poisons coyotes around here." She could feel the fear clamping off her wind, raising her voice to a shriek.

"We're here, Tee. There's Dr. Bradshaw."

Trish had the back doors open even before the van came to a complete stop. She and Amy leaped to the ground at the same instant and turned to lift the muddy blue tarp, easing the dog over the bumper.

"Right through here." Bradshaw held open the door to his surgery.

Trish blinked against the glare when they side-stepped through the doorway and down the hall, the heavy-laden tarp slung between them.

"Up on the table." He took one corner of the tarp and Marge another. "On three—one, two, three." Together they laid the limp form on the stainless steel examining table. The overhead light glared down, highlighting each clump of mud-clotted fur. Eyes closed, his breathing so shallow it failed to lift his ribs, Caesar lay unconscious.

Trish gently stroked his muzzle, whispering encouragement. She watched the vet apply the stethoscope to the once snowy chest. He moved it under the front leg.

"He's still alive, but barely. From the looks of him, I'd say poison. Let's get an IV started and then I'll draw some blood. See if we can figure out what they used."

Trish held the leg as the vet clipped the hair and swabbed a pink patch. While her body did what he requested, her mind bombarded the gates of heaven for her dog.

An hour later Caesar opened his eyes and whimpered deep in his throat. Trish heard him only because she stood crouched over the table by his head. The tip of his tail whisked an inch on the metal surface.

"Easy, old man," she whispered around the knot in her throat. "You're gonna make it, you gotta." She smoothed the short hairs back in front of his ears.

"We'll put him back in a kennel now," the vet said ·hile applying the stethoscope again. "He sounds stronger. The next twenty-four hours will tell the tale."

"Can't we take him home? I'll watch him real careful." Trish kept her eyes on the collie. She knew if she looked up at the vet, she'd cry.

"Trish, you know he's better off here in case he needs emergency procedures." Dr. Bradshaw laid a hand on her shoulder. "I promise to take good care of him."

"I—I know." She stroked the top of Caesar's head, doing her best to tell her dog how much she loved him in the language he knew best. "You don't think someone poisoned him deliberately"—she raised her gaze to meet the doctor's and swallowed—"do you?"

CHAPTER SIX

Dr. Bradshaw nodded his head. "I'm afraid I do."

"Maybe he got into some rat poisoning . . . or . . . or coyote bait, or. . . ." Trish couldn't think of anything else.

"But you say he never leaves the farm. Have you put out any such substances?"

Trish shook her head.

"Then I imagine it was doctored meat left where he would find it. He didn't eat very much or he'd have been dead for sure."

"But—but why? Why a dog? He never hurt anybody!" Trish tore her gaze from the vet's and swung around to find Amy studying her, compassion evident in her blue eyes.

"Parks will come by in the morning for a statement. I think—I'm afraid this was a warning." Amy shook her head. "And maybe this was accidental. As soon as the lab analyzes the bloodwork we'll know what we're up against. At this point we have to cover all the possibilities. My job is to keep you safe, Trish." She turned back to the vet. "Will there be someone here all night?"

The doctor nodded.

"Good then, let's move him and we'll head home."

Together they hoisted the tarp and, with Marge carrying the intravenous bag, transported Caesar back to the kennels. Dr. Bradshaw transferred the dog to the wire cage, laying him on some shredded newspaper. He hung the IV pouch on the door and stepped back so Trish could tell Caesar good-night.

Trish bit her lip to keep the tears from taking over. "You do what he says now, you hear, old boy?" Caesar blinked but didn't open his eyes. "I'll see you tomorrow." She dropped a kiss on his muzzle and stepped back so the vet could close the cage.

"You'll call us if . . ." She couldn't say the words. He *had* to get better.

"Of course. But I think we're on the right track."

Trish dashed the backs of her fingers across her eyes. "Thanks."

By the time she fell into bed hours later, they'd discussed the situation until her mind felt like a tangled skein of yarn. She thumped her pillow and flipped over on her other side. If only she could snap a switch and turn off her mind like she did the lamp.

The old rabbit race persisted around the tracks in her head. If God loved them, why didn't He protect them better? But if God wasn't protecting them, maybe someone in the family would have been hurt! Could God keep the animals safe? If He hadn't been, Caesar would probably be dead by now. She ended up by ordering her rabbits back to their burrows and focused on her three things to be thankful for. Number one: Caesar was still alive and improving. She thought about the word *improving*. Was he? And wasn't this one of those times like her father said, when you thanked God for the outcome in advance, going on faith that He was making it so? She sucked in a deep breath and let it all out, clear to the bottom of her lungs. The warmth seeping into her body felt like a warm bath but without the wet.

Number two was easy. Thanks for Amy. And for winning at the track, for a safe flight for David, for his coming home for the weekend. . . . Trish drifted off on her litany of praise.

First thing in the morning she called the vet. When he said Caesar was much stronger, she jigged in place to let some of the joy escape before she bounced on the ceiling like a runaway balloon. After sharing her news with Marge and Amy, she danced down the hall to take her shower. Caesar was mending. Now all was right with her world.

The phone rang just before Trish opened the door to leave for school. She reached for it but stopped when Amy grabbed it first and frowned at her. "Oops," she grimaced and flinched. She always answered the phone. How would she remember not to?

"Runnin' On Farm." Amy waited, poised with pencil in hand. "Of course. I'll get her for you." She covered the receiver with her hand. "Wait to answer until I pick up the other line, okay?"

Trish nodded and reached for the phone. The wink Amy gave her pushed her curiosity button to full alert. When she heard the click on the line, she said, "Hi, this is Trish."

"Trish, this is Sandra Cameron from the Public Relations Department of Chrysler Corporation in Detroit. How are you today?"

"Fine." Trish's curiosity button turned neon.

"I'm sure you're curious as to why I'm calling."

"Ah, yes." What an understatement.

"Mainly I'd like to set up an interview with you. We could bounce some ideas around. Would that be possible?"

"Sure." The neon button turned into a flashing strobe light.

"How about tomorrow? I can hop a plane and be there about eleven."

"I have school." Trish felt her tongue stumbling over her teeth. What was going on?

"I think this is important enough you'll want to miss a couple of hours. Please make sure your mother can be there also. Will this be all right?"

Trish mumbled an assent and then gave directions from the airport before gaining the courage to ask, "What's this all about?"

"I'd really rather wait until we can talk face-to-face. I'll see you tomorrow about eleven. Oh, and here's my number in case there's a problem."

When Trish hung up the phone she understood what being run over by a steamroller felt like. What in the world was going on? She stared out the window down toward the barns. A thought teased the back of her mind but refused to be identified.

"You really don't know what that's about?" Amy asked from the front door.

"Not a bit." Trish headed down the hall and knocked on the bathroom door, where she could hear the shower running, before sticking her head inside the steamy room. "I'm outa here. Oh, and, Mom, you gonna be home tomorrow about eleven?"

"I think so, why?"

"A Sandra Cameron called from the Chrysler Corporation—wants to meet with us."

The shower stopped. Marge peeked out the shower door. "What?"

"Gotta go. Love you." Trish shut the door on her mother's "Tricia Marie Evanston!"

"You know anything about that?" Amy asked when they drove down the lane.

"Not really." Trish shrugged. "Guess we'll find out tomorrow." What was it she couldn't remember?

When they picked up Rhonda they brought her up to speed on all the excitement.

"I'm so glad Caesar's better. I prayed for him all night."

"All night?" Trish glanced in the rearview mirror to check out her friend's face.

"Well, every time I woke up. Seemed like all night. So you see this Detroit lady tomorrow?"

"Yeah . . . wish I knew what it was about. The suspense is killing me."

"It's about the advertising campaign, you know, the one that reporter down in San Mateo told you about. They want you to—"

"That's it! The thing I've been trying to remember." Trish thumped her hand on the steering wheel. "How do you think he knew about this? That was weeks ago." None of them came up with any answers, just more questions, by the time they arrived at Prairie High School.

Trish dropped her things off at her locker and stopped at the front desk just as the second bell rang. "I need to talk to Mrs. Olson," she told the student working the counter. "She's my advisor," she whispered to Amy.

"You better ask for the principal too," Amy replied.

"I need to talk with both of them."

By the time the meeting was over, Trish remembered how little kids felt when grown-ups talked about them as if they weren't there. They could at least have asked her opinion rather than planning her life for her.

"Sorry about that," Amy said as they headed for first period. "It just seemed to work faster if I handled it." Trish muttered her agreement. "But from now on, I'm just your favorite cousin from Spokane, right?"

"Right."

"I forgot to tell them about the gift money from TBA." Trish smacked her forehead with the heel of her hand. "Now I'll have to stay after school to catch them."

"Would now be better?"

"No, we're late enough for class as it is." Trish didn't need Nagger to call her names. She was doing a good enough job of that all on her lonesome. She retrieved her things from her locker and headed for class.

The boys at their lunch table reacted to Amy with the same drop-the-jaw expression David and Brad had adopted. Trish and Rhonda swapped their *oh-brother* looks and kept from giggling by sheer willpower.

"Should I tell them the bad news—that she's engaged?" Trish whispered behind her hand.

Rhonda shook her head. "Naw, let them suffer later. Serves 'em right." She glared at Jason Wollensvaldt, a foreign exchange student from Germany and her somewhat boyfriend, who looked as star struck as the rest.

———

Mrs. Olson and Mr. Patterson, the principal, kept Trish waiting for an extra fifteen minutes after school before they could see her. Counting the seconds as the clock ticked them off did nothing to calm her twitching fingers. If only she had the vet's number with her. But by the time she decided to head for the pay phone with a phone book, they beckoned her into the office.

Trish laid the check on the desk in front of the man whose shoulders were as broad as his forehead was bare. He tipped his head to peer through horn-rimmed bifocals. "What in the world?" He looked at Trish, question marks all over his face, while handing the paper to Mrs. Olson.

Mrs. Olson read it and grinned. "Okay, Trish, come clean. What's going on here?"

Trish sat forward on the edge of her seat. "Like it?"

"Of course." Patterson leaned back, his hands clasped behind his head. "But what did we do to deserve $1,000?"

"It's in thanks for the work Prairie kids did to collect signatures. I was going to give it to you this morning but I forgot."

"Well." Mrs. Olson picked up the check and studied it again. "Did they make any recommendations for how we use it?" Trish shook her head. Mrs. Olson shifted her gaze to the principal. "Then I think the government class that started all this should vote on how it's put to use. Agreed?"

Mr. Patterson massaged the shiny front part of his scalp with beefy hands. "Don't see why not. That should be another good lesson in government by the people. What do you think, Trish?"

"You mean it?" She could feel a grin cracking her cheekbones.

"Yes, and I think you should be the one to tell them."

"Really?" She caught herself just before sliding off

the chair. "Even Ms. Wainwright?" At their nods, she slapped the arms of the chair. "All right!" Trish jumped to her feet. "I'll tell them in class tomorrow. What a blast that'll be!" She headed for the door, only pausing to beckon, "Come on, Amy, we've got stuff to do."

Trish opened the glass-windowed door. "Oh, no! I won't be here tomorrow." She spun back around. "That woman from Chrysler is coming."

"Then you'll have to tell them Wednesday." Mrs. Olson rose to her feet. "You can handle the secret for one more day, can't you?"

"I guess." Trish rolled her eyes and shrugged. "But it won't be easy."

"Good things never are." Mrs. Olson patted Trish's shoulder. "We'll get a thank-you letter off immediately. Pick up the check to show the class after lunch on Wednesday, all right?"

Trish nodded again. "Thanks." And out the door they went.

As soon as Trish walked in the front door back at Runnin' On Farm, she called the vet. "Caesar's been drinking water on his own," she announced. "Vet says he maybe can come home tomorrow if he continues like this." She executed a jig step to the refrigerator. "Amy, you want something to drink?"

The warm glow stayed in her middle while she changed clothes and headed for the barns. Patrick would be at the track feeding the racing string and someone had to take care of the home stock. Amy carried her can of soda with her.

———

Trish breathed both a sigh and a prayer of relief that

night when she snuggled down under the covers. They hadn't heard a peep from the stalker. That was the good news. The bad news? She couldn't get him out of her mind. Where—and how would he strike next?

She woke in the morning feeling like Nagger had been going at her all night—with his foot to the floorboards. Here she was beginning to think he'd moved on to pester someone else. The vacation had been grand.

She rubbed her eyes with both hands, then dragged the same through her tangled hair. Even the sheet and blankets were wrapped around her legs as if they'd been the opposing side in a free-for-all. She lay still a moment trying to remember what she'd been dreaming about. Nothing. Just this heavy feeling in the pit of her stomach and a pounding headache.

Caesar! She jerked her feet from the binding covers and sprinted down the hall. Good thing they had the veterinarian's number on speed dial. She punched four and drummed her fingers on the counter, waiting for an answer. When she looked at the clock, it only registered six-thirty.

"Come on, be there."

The answering machine kicked in. Trish groaned and dropped the receiver in the hook, fishing for the phone book under the counter with her other hand. His home number was listed in their file at the front of the book. She dialed again.

When he answered, she could hardly keep the quiver from her voice. "Dr. Bradshaw, this is Trish Evanston. Is Caesar all right?"

"Far as I know. He was so much stronger last night I planned to release him today, just like I told you. What's the matter?"

Trish shook her head. "I don't know. I—I just had this awful feeling." She stumbled over her words, all the while calling herself names inside her head. "Sorry I bothered you."

As Trish hung up the phone Marge stepped out of the bathroom, pink towel wrapped around her head. "Trish, are you all right?"

Trish rubbed her aching temples. "I guess. I—I'm not sure." She took the aspirin bottle from the cupboard and poured two tablets into her palm. After downing the pills with a glass of water, she leaned on her arms over the sink.

Marge came up behind her and felt her daughter's forehead. "No temp. Any other symptoms?"

Trish shook her head, which only accelerated the beat of the bass drum echoing in her skull. "Patrick okay?"

Marge nodded.

"All the horses?"

"Far as I know. Trish, what in the world . . ."

Trish started to shake her head and caught herself just in time. "Where's Amy?"

"She had to meet with Officer Parks. She went early so she could be back in time for school. Tee, you're scaring me. What is this?"

"Wish I knew, Mom. Just bad dreams, I guess." She rubbed her forehead. "Think I'll lie down for a couple more minutes." She shrugged, her half-attempted smile more a grimace. "Don't worry. Everything'll be okay, right?"

All the way down the hall she placed each foot in front of the other with deliberate care, in order to keep the drum from deepening its beat. Lying down with the same degree of caution wasn't easy with the twisted covers, but she managed.

"Here." Marge laid a cold washcloth across Trish's forehead just after her head nestled into the pillow.

"Thanks."

"Remember, you have that appointment with what's-her-name from Chrysler."

Trish winced. She kept herself from shaking her head again. "I know."

Marge tucked the covers around her daughter's shoulders. "You want to skip first period or even stay home?"

"No, call me in fifteen minutes. I'll be better." And she was.

After taking a quick shower, she felt almost human again. What had gotten into her?

"I think you're psychic," Rhonda answered after Trish told her tale in the car on the way to school.

"Rhonda!" Trish clenched her fingers around the steering wheel. "Whatever made you think of something like that? I had a bad dream and woke up so tense I got a headache. No big deal!"

"I read about some guy who could, you know, pick up the vibes or something. They called it . . ." She paused. "Ummm . . ."

"Precognition?" Amy questioned from the second seat. "I've heard that many people have it but some only sporadically." She leaned forward. "But what I read said most people don't believe in such a thing. I agree with Trish—she had a bad night. There's enough stuff been going on around here to give anyone a bad night. Dreams sometime just reflect what's going on inside of us . . . help our psyche work it all out."

"Huh?" Rhonda turned in her seat. "Care to run that by me again?"

"It just means . . ."

"Let's drop it, okay? Talk about something upbeat."

"How's Caesar?"

"Better. We can pick him up this afternoon."

"And your meeting with the fancy car lady?"

"Thanks for nothing. Now my butterflies are trying to race each other out my throat." Trish swung the car into the parking lot at the high school. "Rhonda, sometimes I could . . ." She parked the car and set the brake. "If I don't get back to school, you'll need to get a ride home."

"No problema. Jason'll take me home anytime I let him." Rhonda opened the car door at the same moment a certain tall exchange student reached for the handle. She turned and winked at Trish. "See? I told you."

Trish watched her friend laugh up at the blond giant. "They say he's a wizard with a basketball."

"Looks like he knows how to catch a girl too." Amy grinned at Trish in the rearview mirror. "We're going to be late if we don't hustle."

"Yeah." Trish swung open her door and stepped to the ground. Eleven o'clock wasn't very far away either.

CHAPTER SEVEN

Sandra Cameron was late.

Trish glanced at the clock over the sink in the kitchen again. Here she'd rushed home to be on time and now they waited.

"Only ten minutes. You know how it can be renting a car."

"Even if you're a Chrysler executive?"

"Probably even if you were chairman of the board." Amy and Marge clutched matching coffee mugs and leaned against the kitchen counter. "Unless you get a limo, and those have been known to get lost too."

"Voice of experience?" Marge glanced over her shoulder to check the driveway.

"For sure. Cops get escort duty plenty in their beginning years." Amy breathed in the steam rising from her cup. "You sure make a good cup of coffee."

Trish eyed the platter of fresh cinnamon rolls sitting on the counter. "Wait 'til you taste her specialty." As if looking through a telescope, she watched her fingers drumming on the counter. The rhythm matched that of the butterflies fluttering in her midsection. Feeling the urge for the second time since arriving home, she headed down the hall to the bathroom. Did nerves affect everyone this way? She'd just flushed the toilet when Marge knocked on the door.

"She's here, Tee."

Trish dashed her hands under the water, made a face at the one she saw in the mirror, and finished drying her hands on her pants when she walked back down the hall. Through the front window she could see a tall, corporate-suit-clad woman retrieving her briefcase from the front seat of a black LeBaron. She tossed back her shoulder-length pageboy hair and strode up the walk.

Trish swallowed to wet her dry throat. Was this really about her being in an advertisement, or did they want to take her cars back? Maybe they thought three red convertibles were too many for one person. Her mother motioned toward the front door, obviously meaning for Trish to answer it. Having her feet glued to the floor made forward locomotion difficult.

When the knock sounded, Trish ripped her feet from their moorings and, pasting what she hoped looked like a smile on her face, answered the door.

"Tricia Evanston?" The woman extended her manicured hand. "I'm Sandra Cameron. How are you today?"

"F-fine." Trish swallowed again and gestured for the woman to enter. *You sound like an idiot, Evanston.* Thank God for mothers.

Marge greeted the woman, making the small talk that grown-ups did so well and that Trish felt tongue-tied over. Give her horses to talk about anytime and she did fine, but gosh, this woman was from . . .

Trish took herself sternly in hand. If she could talk easily over a microphone to thousands of fans at the track, surely she could handle this interview. After all, it didn't really mean anything—did it?

By this time Marge had them all sitting comfortably in the living room while she exited to the kitchen for the coffee.

"So now, how are things going with your racing?" Sandra leaned forward on the sofa and clasped her hands together on her knees.

"Good." Trish flashed her a grin. "We opened at Portland Meadows on Saturday."

"I hear you won the Hal Evanston Memorial Cup."

"You did?" Trish's voice squeaked on the "did."

"Trish, I don't think you know what a celebrity you are. Sunday's paper in Detroit carried a big article about all your efforts to keep the track open and then winning the cup in memory of your father."

Trish gritted her teeth against the flash of tears behind her eyelids. One sniff and she was fine again.

"No, I guess not."

"Curt Donovan is making quite a name for himself writing about the 'Comeback Kid.'" Sandra pulled a sheaf of articles, paper-clipped together, from her briefcase and handed them across the open space. "See?"

Trish glanced down at the picture of her accepting the trophy, then looked back up at her guest. "Wow—I mean, I knew this was in our papers but clear back in Detroit?" She shrugged. "It wasn't like I was at Churchill Downs or something."

"But you will be soon, right?"

"Sure, we're running Firefly in the Oaks, and I'm riding for Bob Diego in the Breeder's Cup."

"But not Spitfire."

"I wish. But the syndicate would never let me. He's too valuable at stud now."

"How about if we make him a movie star too?"

"What?"

"Well at least a star model. We at Chrysler would like you and Spitfire to star in a series of ads we've designed for LeBaron convertibles. We'll shoot them at BlueMist Farms, since we already checked and they don't want to transport him off the farm if they can help it. I know this is tight timing, but we'd like to spend three days shooting—hopefully we can finish in that time—beginning on Monday next week. You'd fly to Lexington on Sunday, shoot Monday, Tuesday, and Wednesday, and have Thursday off before you race on Friday. What do you think?"

The shiver started at her toes and worked its way up. Star in an ad? Whoa!

"Don't you think that big black horse of yours would look great beside a bright red convertible? And the camera loves you. We know that from all the pictures we've seen, both TV and print."

Trish tried to find words. She really did. They just wouldn't come.

"We'll pay you, of course. And pay for the use of Spitfire also." She named an exorbitant figure. "And if this works like we think it will, you'd continue to be a spokesperson for Chrysler. Usually we'd make all the arrangements with your agent, but since you don't have one . . ."

Trish shot her mother a look of pure pleading.

"Trish has an agent." Marge set her tray down on the coffee table.

"I know she has one at the tracks, but this would be

entirely different. All the big names in sports, film, or modeling have agents to help build their careers." Sandra accepted the coffee and cinnamon roll. "Thanks. This looks delicious."

Trish used the moment to shake her mind out of total shock and unlock her tongue. She looked over at Amy, sitting so quietly by the window, and caught a wink that helped bring her back to the mission at hand. *They want me and Spitfire to star in ads—for Chrysler. We can do that—can't we? Sure we can. No big deal—right?* She rolled her lips together to stifle the giggles that threatened to erupt. *Wait 'til Rhonda hears this. She'll freak. Totally freak!*

Ms. Cameron's voice brought Trish back to the living room with a thump. "I know I've been doing all the talking. Marge, these cinnamon rolls are simply scrumptious. So Trish, I'd like to hear what you think of all this. Are you interested?"

Am I interested? Do horses eat grass? Trish sucked in a deep breath and let it all out. This was supposed to help her relax. Could she count on her voice to work now?

"I g-guess." *Yeah, right. I sound like a total idiot.* She tried again. "I think this sounds exciting—like I never dreamed of such a thing."

"Then you're interested?" At Trish's nod, Sandra smiled and leaned back against the sofa. "Good. Then we can proceed."

They talked for another hour before Sandra asked, "How about if I take you all out for lunch? I need to call my boss and tell him this is a go, so if I could use your phone?" At Marge's nod, Sandra rose to her feet. "While I'm doing that, why don't you keep thinking of any questions you have. Also if you have an attorney you'd like to discuss this with, have him look over the contract."

Amy came over to sit on the stone hearth to be by Trish. "Wait 'til I tell 'em down at headquarters about sitting in at a meeting like this. Trish, this is absolutely fantastic! I can't begin to tell you how thrilled I am for you."

"Pinch me to make sure I'm not dreaming." Trish held out her arm. "Ouch, guess I'm not." She leaned forward in her father's recliner. "Mom, what do you think? You've been awfully quiet."

"Just wishing your father were here to see all this. He'd be so proud." A tear meandered down her cheek till she swiped it away with the tips of her fingers.

"You'll go too?" Trish blinked against the moisture threatening to overspill.

"Of course. Just never thought I'd be a stage mother. Course I never planned on being the mother of a celebrity at all." She shook her head. "Life is strange all right."

"Couldn't happen to better people." Amy leaned back against the stone fireplace. "Just couldn't."

"You think God wants me to do this?" Trish turned again to her mother.

"If not, He'll close the doors. That's how I've been praying." Marge took her daughter's hand in hers. "I always pray for His perfect will and what is best for you."

"You two are something else." Amy leaned forward, hands on her knees.

"What do you mean?"

"I don't think I've ever seen real faith in action like I have here. Makes me want it too."

"Okay, that's all taken care of." Sandra walked back across the room. Her smile included them all. "We're really pleased with your agreement. Really pleased. The wheels are now in motion, not that they weren't before."

Trish clenched her hands together. *Wow! Is God working or is God working? Like Dad always said, "Walking the walk is a better witness than just talking the talk."* She shot an arrow prayer heavenward for Amy.

"Now, do you have a favorite restaurant?" Sandra stopped before the trio at the fireplace, as if aware she'd interrupted something. "You want me to go out and come back in a while?"

Marge shook her head. "No, this has nothing to do with our discussions. Diamond Lil's is nice, has good food." She laid a hand on Trish's shoulder. "Unless you'd rather have Trish's favorite."

"Pizza."

"I *was* thinking of something a little fancier than that."

Within minutes they were all four piled into the minivan and heading down the driveway. They waved at Patrick returning from the track in the pickup.

By the time they were seated at the restaurant and had ordered, Trish had a multitude of questions bubbling over. Things like: what lines to say, what she'd be wearing, what scenes they'd thought of, what a "shoot" was like, when would the TV spots air?

Sandra held up her hand. "Easy, I won't remember all the questions. How about if I just run through what a typical day might be like. Keep in mind, though, that Murphy's Law is nowhere more proved out than on a commercial shoot."

"Murphy's Law?" Trish wrinkled her eyebrows.

"You know, what can go wrong will go wrong." Sandra picked up a breadstick and smeared the tip in a pat of butter. She waved it in the air before crunching a bite. "Never fails."

"Oh." Trish reached for her own breadstick.

By the time they'd finished eating and Sandra finished talking, Trish had that becoming-familiar steamrollered feeling. What in the world possessed her to think she could pretend to be a model or an actress? While Amy and Sandra finished another cup of coffee, Trish and her mother read and reread the contract.

"What I'd like you to do is drop this off at your attorney's before we return to the farm for my car and he can go over it. You can sign it tomorrow in his office and fax me a copy, then send the real thing by overnight mail. Since you're a minor, Trish, your mother has to sign all of them too. I'll call you with a couple of names for agents if you'd like after I get back to the office."

"Do I really need one?"

"Depends on if you want to parley your popularity into more endorsements or not. They can give you good advice too."

"Why don't you see how you like this before we go any further," Marge advised. "It's not like you don't already have plenty to do. School has to come first."

"I know."

"We're required by law to have a tutor on the set for minors still in school."

"I can keep up. It's not like I'm going to be gone for months or anything." Trish could feel her old resentment flare. Her mother was showing her worryitis again. With her, school and good grades were most important, almost next to praying. What if her daughter decided *not* to attend college? Or at least postpone it?

Trish tamped down the thoughts. They didn't need an argument right now.

By the time they arrived back at Runnin' On Farm, the sun was heading for its nest in the west. Trish felt herself getting impatient. She had planned to pick Caesar up right after school. Brad's baby blue Mustang occupied its usual place in the turnaround in front of the house. He would be down doing chores. Patrick would be at the track again, feeding and putting the racing string to bed.

Even so, the entire place seemed empty without Caesar barking his welcome.

Sandra bid them all goodbye and left with a promise to talk with them the next day.

Trish heaved a sigh of relief. Right now she needed a bit of calm to recover from all the excitement.

"Kind of like a whirlwind, isn't she?" Amy joined Trish on her march to the house.

"I guess."

Trish opened the front door and turned left to the kitchen while Amy headed down the hall, stopping in the bathroom.

Brad had dropped the mail on the counter, so Trish began leafing through, hoping for a letter from Red. Instead a small brown package sported her name. She took a knife from the drawer and sliced the tape, surprised at how heavy it was.

What would anyone be sending her?

She undid the paper and pulled the top off the tan box. Inside lay a brick with a note taped to it.

Trish felt and heard her shriek at the same instant.

CHAPTER EIGHT

"Trish!" Amy barreled across the living room.

Trish stared at the package as if it contained live rattlesnakes. "Bang! You're dead!" the letters on the note stated plainly.

Amy first checked out Trish to see if she'd been injured, then transferred her attention to the box on the counter. "It coulda been a bomb," she muttered under her breath. She spun around and pinned Trish to the refrigerator with a glare tipped in ice. "Why ever did you open it? I told you to let me check any letters—that's it!" She slammed her palm on the counter so hard the box jumped.

"It—it wasn't a letter and I was so—so happy I didn't even think about—about—you know. I just thought someone sent me a present, maybe Red—or—somebody." Trish couldn't keep from stammering. Or shaking either. She'd been having such fun and now this!

"Whatever is going on?" Marge charged through the door and skidded to a stop. "Oh, dear God, now what?"

"Let me set you both straight." Amy's voice slashed like a whip. "Let *me* open the mail, answer the phone, get the door. How can I get this through your heads? Some kook is out there trying to scare the daylights out of you . . ."

"He's doing a bang-up job of it." Trish wrapped her arms around her middle. She felt as if she'd stepped outside in the middle of an ice storm.

"Right. And maybe he has more than scaring you in mind." Amy's voice softened and she drew Trish into her arms. "Hey, buddy, I've come to care for you more than a little. You have to be careful—and let me do my job."

Trish bit her lip. She *would not* cry. But it was easier to keep the tears back when Amy was yelling at her.

"Would someone please tell me what is going on here?" Marge stared from Amy to Trish and back again.

"You tell her." Trish pulled away and jerked a tissue out of the box by the phone. She blew her nose and wiped her eyes. "I'm going after Caesar."

"No you're not. I'm calling Parks and he'll be right out to talk with us."

"He can wait. Caesar is more important right now. He's been waiting all day." She snatched her purse off the counter and headed for the door.

"Trish, you can't go alone." Marge snagged her purse, shot Amy a look of apology, and followed Trish to the van. "I'll drive home so you can stay in the back with Caesar. Otherwise he'll be all over the car, and he's still too weak for that."

Trish shoved the key into the ignition and waited for her mother to get in. "All I did was open a package addressed to me. And no, I didn't look to see who sent it— I was having too good a time. There must be a law somewhere against Trish Evanston having fun."

Trish drove the car down the drive and out on the

road, and still her mother didn't reply. "Well? Aren't you going to yell at me too?"

"No. You're doing too good a job of that yourself." Marge fastened her seat belt. Trish looked over at her mother when she heard the snap of the belt. Her words sounded calm but the two lines between her eyebrows furrowed deeper. Trish could tell she was worried.

But then, who wouldn't be?

Most of the shaking had subsided by the time they pulled into the parking lot of the veterinary clinic. When Trish glanced at her mother, she received an almost smile in return. "At least we can thank God Caesar is getting better."

"And that you weren't hurt. When I think of that mail bomb that blew a man's hand off not too long ago—Tee, I'm just grateful you're only mad."

Trish shook her head. "Let's go get the dog."

Caesar struggled to his feet when he saw her and heard her voice. His tail feathered only a bit, but at least he was wagging it. When she opened his cage, he tottered a step forward and made sure her face got a requisite cleaning.

"You old silly, you." Trish tugged on his ruff and rumpled his ears. When just those actions made him waver, she turned to look at Dr. Bradshaw. "You sure he's okay to take home?"

"I'm sure. He'll get better faster there with those he loves. Just keep him in the house or a kennel."

"No kennel. We'll make him a bed by the back door."

"Make sure he has water all the time and if he quits voiding, bring him back in. That means his kidneys are in trouble. You might have to help him outside."

"That's fine, then." Marge shifted her purse to the

other shoulder. "Trish, we need to get home."

Trish stepped back from the front of the cage so the vet could lift Caesar and carry him out to the car. She ran ahead to open the back door and climb in. When Dr. Bradshaw laid Caesar with his head in her lap, she smiled her thanks and buried her face in the dog's ruff. Caesar licked her nose once, then sighed. His tail thumped against the wheel well.

"Yeah, I'm glad to see you too, even if you do smell of disinfectant."

But she wasn't so glad to see the patrol car and Curt Donovan's white newspaper car parked in their yard. "More questions," she muttered. "If I never answer another policeman's questions, it'll be too soon." Caesar thumped his tail. When the door opened to the face of a strange man, the dog bared his teeth and rumbled low in his throat.

"Tell him it's okay." Officer Parks stepped back. "I just want to carry him in. He's too heavy for you."

"Hey, fella, it's okay. Parks is our friend." Trish's voice slipped into the croon she used on the horses with the same calming effect. Caesar allowed himself to be picked up in the officer's strong arms, and with Trish right by his side, her hand on his head, entered the house to a hero's welcome.

Brad, Patrick, Curt, and Amy gathered around while Trish grabbed a blanket from the closet and pulled a rug over to pad the bed for the weary dog. He lay down with a sigh, but as soon as Trish tried to move away, he scrabbled and lurched to his feet.

"Easy, fella, you stay there." But when her words had no effect, Trish sank down beside the dog. "Guess you'll have to question me right here."

They went over the events of the package opening three times with nothing new coming up.

"I'll take the package in for fingerprinting and see if we can't determine which post office it came from—see if anyone remembers anything." Parks shook his head. "Whoever this is has to make a mistake pretty soon. Or he's a lot smarter than I think he is."

"All they have to do nowadays is watch TV," Patrick grumbled. "With all the crime and police shows, a body can learn to commit about any kind of crime. Don't take a genius."

"Could this be a copycat crime?" Curt asked. "Since Highstreet doesn't seem to have anything to do with it?"

"Could be. Highstreet would have a hard time. We've tapped his phone and have him under constant surveillance. He can't blow his nose without us knowing."

"Fat lot of good it seems to be doing." Trish continued stroking her sleeping dog's head.

"Yeah, cases like this don't get solved in one hour, like on TV. Welcome to the real world of police work—patience and persistence." Parks accepted the mug of coffee Marge offered. "Most cases are solved only through hours and weeks of digging out one detail after another."

"Amen to that." Amy joined Trish on the floor beside the collie. She ran a hand over the dog's side and shook her head. "Boy, he lost a lot of weight. Wait 'til I get my hands on that—"

"We're not sure if Caesar's poisoning is connected to this case or not," Parks reminded her. "He could have just picked up some bad meat."

Amy shook her head, sending her blond hair flying. "My women's intuition says guilty." She raised a hand, palm out. "No, don't you go shaking your head. How many times have I been right on?" She grinned at his pained expression. "Bugs you, doesn't it?"

"Well, I better get back to the track to feed. Brad— you coming with me or doing those here?" Patrick pushed back his chair. "Thanks for the coffee. Good as usual." He picked his hat off the counter.

"I'll stay here." Brad exchanged looks with Patrick. "Keep an eye out."

The phone rang and at Amy's glare, Trish didn't even begin to get to her feet. The police officer gave Caesar a farewell pat and stood. When she headed for the phone, Trish laid her cheek on Caesar's head. She could feel her pulse pounding, all at the ringing of the telephone. What a mess.

"Trish, it's Rhonda." Amy stuck her head around the corner of the refrigerator. "How about if you call her back?" Trish nodded. Rhonda would freak for sure when she heard this latest news.

After Parks and Curt left, Trish and Amy joined Brad down at the barns. While Marge worked the babies in the morning, Trish trained the two almost-two-year-olds in the afternoon. They were to be ready for the track sometime after the first of the year. Late as it was, all the horses, from broodmares and young stock to old Dan'l, lined the fences of their paddocks, waiting for their treats.

"That's some picture." Amy took several pieces of carrot from Trish's bucket. "Being here with you and the horses is going to make any other assignment stale by comparison."

"You're welcome to visit anytime." Trish whistled just for the pleasure of hearing the responding nickers. Old Dan'l let loose with a full-blown whinny, tossing his head enough to set his gray mane flying.

"You want to ride him?" Trish asked when she fed the babies their treats. "Easy now, Miss Tee." She grabbed the filly's halter. "You know better than to shove like that."

"Dan'l?" Amy sneaked Double Diamond a second carrot chunk.

Trish nodded.

"You mean it?"

"You said you know how to ride."

"I do. Rode for years before I went away to college." She gave the youngster a last pat. "You be good now, you hear?" The colt nodded and rubbed his forehead against her shoulder, leaving white hairs on her navy sweatshirt. Amy pushed his head away with a chuckle. "What a lover."

Trish did the same with Miss Tee. "Yeah, these two ought to be really something about a year from now. Since Miss Tee was born last September, she'll be running a year late."

"This thing about all thoroughbreds having their birthday on January first doesn't make a lot of sense to me."

"Me either, but they have to have some sort of guidelines. Would be pretty confusing otherwise." She gave the mares their treats and requisite pats. Dan'l nickered again and pawed the grass. "I'm coming. Hold on to your shorts." The gray only tossed his head and nickered louder.

"I think he likes you." Amy stuck her hands in her back pockets. "Talk about a peaceful scene."

"I know. My dad used to come out here in the evenings just to enjoy the horses and the quiet. Said it was his special time. Mornings were always too hectic what with works at the track and all."

"From what everyone tells me, he was a pretty special guy."

"Yep." Trish buried her face in Dan'l's mane. Would she ever be able to talk about her father without the tears burning her eyes? She gave the old gray another carrot and stroked his face from forelock to quivering nostrils. His munching filled the silence. A crow cawed from the top of a fir tree, joining the chorus of the peeper frogs from the creek.

Trish watched Amy scan the area, checking out the sounds and the silences, before returning her gaze to Trish with a smile.

Trish sighed. Amy was ever the police officer, keeping on top of her job. The thought of being the focus of that job made her stomach knot. Someone wouldn't invade her life here, would they? She snagged her thoughts back from the black well and concentrated on the warm, gray body beside her. "Well, old fellow, how would you like a turn or two around the track?" She snapped the lead onto his halter. "I'm sure Brad has those two ready to run . . . probably wondering what happened to us."

A shiver ran up her back. What if there really was someone out there watching them?

Trish couldn't shake the unease all through the gallops with the two horses in training. She forced herself to pay attention, working the colt through his paces, forcing herself not to look over her shoulder. Keeping her eyes on his ears rather than the trees across the track. Listening for changes in breathing that told of his fitness rather than listening for strange noises.

Bang! You're dead! The words of the note flew up before her eyes when she blinked. It would be so easy for someone to take a shot at them.

What if he hurt one of the horses? The thought clamped off her air.

By the time they finished, she couldn't keep her hands from shaking.

"What's wrong?" Brad took the brush from her hands. He turned her square to him so he could look right in her face.

Amy ducked under the colt's neck, leaving her brushing job. "You okay?"

Trish shook her head. "I can't get that note out of my mind. All of a sudden I realized how open we are here." She glanced over her shoulder. "Those trees and all. I've never been afraid in my own home before." She clenched and unclenched her fists. "I hate him. What kind of rotten person would do such a thing?"

Brad gathered her in his arms and, after taking off her helmet, stroked her hair. "Easy, Tee. Amy's here to watch for that. It'll be okay."

"No it won't." Trish clamped the front of his shirt in her fists. "Nothing'll ever be the same again."

———

That night in bed, she flipped from side to side trying to get comfortable. Knowing Caesar lay by the back door didn't really help. Up until now she hadn't realized how much she depended on him to warn them of people coming on the farm. *Of course, you idiot. You didn't worry about anything before. You always thought you were safe.* She called herself a few other names as she flipped over again. No dad, no dog—well, not quite, but out of commission for a time at least.

A knock sounded on her door. "Trish, are you all right?" Her mother poked her head in. "I could hear you tossing around."

"I'm just fine."

"Right. And I'm Mother Theresa." Marge sat down on the edge of the bed. "What's happening?"

Trish slammed her pillows in place behind her head and propped herself up. "I hate that man—person— whoever is doing this to us."

"I'm not surprised."

"Well, don't you?"

"I'm trying not to."

"I hate being scared. I've never been afraid like this in my entire life." Trish crossed her arms over her chest. "People shouldn't have to be scared in their own homes."

"Or anywhere else, for that matter." Marge brought one knee up on the bedspread, turning to face her daughter. "You know God has promised to watch over us. What's that song, 'His eye is on the sparrow . . .'?"

"Yeah, well, all I've felt this afternoon is eyes on me. Don't think I want anymore."

"You don't mean that." Marge reached over and smoothed back a lock of wavy black hair from her daughter's forehead.

"Maybe if I felt God's eyes, I'd feel better."

"Have you been praying for this person?"

Trish gave a snort that more than answered her mother's question.

"You want me to pray with you?"

This snort was even more descriptive.

Marge leaned forward and dropped a kiss on Trish's cheek. "I'll pray, but keep in mind that praying for those who hate us makes us feel better. Good-night, Tee."

Pray for him. Right! "Okay, God, here's the deal—you get him before I do."

The nightmares struck with a vengeance.

CHAPTER NINE

Trish sat straight up in bed, her heart pounding as if she'd run a mile. She stared into the corners of her room, half expecting the man who'd been chasing her to jump out of the darkness. Hand to her thundering heart, she sucked in air, sometimes catching on a sob. Who was he? Why was anyone chasing her? And even in her dreams!

She swung her feet to the floor and padded down the hall to the bathroom. When she heard Caesar whine, she continued on and sank down on the floor beside him. "What do you need, fella?"

His tongue flicked the tip of her nose. When he struggled to stand, she helped him with an arm around his back and rib cage, rising to her knees as he stood. "You need to go outside?" He whined and took a tottering step. The cold night air sent goose bumps racing up her arms when she opened the door. "Let me get a jacket."

Caesar whined again and wobbled toward the door opening. Trish grabbed a coat off the rack and shoved her feet into an old pair of boots her mother used. The dog was half out the door and falling before she caught him. "Silly, I said I'd help you if you could just hang on a minute."

"Everything okay?" Amy appeared at the doorway, belting her robe as she spoke.

Trish nearly dropped the dog. "Good grief, you scared me to bits."

"Sorry." Amy wrapped her arms around Caesar's hindquarters. "Okay, old man, Trish, let's get this potty break over with. My feet are freezing."

Back in the house with Caesar settled on his pad again, Trish led the way down the hall. "And to think a nightmare woke me up. I was just going to the bathroom." She shivered and rubbed her arms. "How come having Caesar helpless like that makes me feel so . . ."

"Helpless yourself?"

"I guess. Hey—don't you ever sleep?"

"Sure. Guess I'm like the scouts in the Old West—learned to sleep with one ear wide awake. Opening doors are a sure-fired signal to set me straight up and out before I even think."

"Sure glad I don't ever have to sneak up on you." Trish shut the bathroom door behind herself. Sometimes Amy helped her feel safer, but other times, like tonight, just brought the idea of danger even closer. "Couldn't have anything to do with my dream, could it?" The face in the mirror made the right moves but never responded. The sound of the flushing toilet seemed unnaturally loud in the nighttime stillness.

Or was it that anything sounded loud tonight?

"Trish, you're going to be late." Marge's voice sounded as if from a long distance.

At the same moment, Trish became aware of the buzzing from her alarm. No wonder she'd been dreaming about bees and being chased—again.

Her feet hit the floor at the same moment her eyes checked the clock. Seven-fifteen! "Why'd you let me sleep so long?" Barreling past her mother, she headed for the bathroom. "Now I'm going to be late." She scrubbed her teeth as if they'd never meet a toothbrush again. No time for a shower, no time for hair—her stomach growled—and no time for breakfast either.

"How's Caesar?" Her question floated behind her on her way back to her room. She grumbled her way through her closet, dressing and finding her tennies. So, she'd slept through her alarm. Wasn't that what mothers were for? Back in the bathroom, she jerked the brush through her hair, wincing at the pain.

Some day *this* was going to be—a bad hair day for sure. Ouch, she couldn't even braid it without snagging.

"Thanks, Mom." The tone said "thanks for nothing" and from the frown on her mother's face, Trish knew she'd read the tone. By the time she'd started the car, Nagger settled himself firmly on her shoulder. *Letting things get to you, aren't you?* Maybe he was half cat; he certainly purred like one. *Thought you were going to copy your dad and give God the glory for everything?*

Trish clamped her bottom lip between her teeth. Maybe if she clamped hard enough, she could drown out that infernal, internal voice. Were consciences supposed to snicker?

Even Amy shot her a raised-eyebrow look when Trish made a dig at Rhonda and her boyfriend. Rhonda's hurt look cut through Trish's bad mood like a chainsaw through cheese.

"Sorry." Trish reached out and caught her friend's arm before she leaped out of the van. "Guess all this is really getting to me."

"Yeah, it is. And your bad attitude is really getting to *me*. Don't bother to wait for me after school. Jason will take me home."

Now you've really blown it. Tisking away, Nagger only made her feel worse. It was all that jerk's fault, whoever he was. Hate was far too mild a word.

Rhonda didn't take her usual place at the lunch table and when Trish tried to find her, she and Jason were sitting at a table clear across the room. For all their years in school, they'd always shared a table. Trish felt as if half herself was missing. All the football players, including Doug, flirted with Amy, leaving Trish to drown in her puddle of self-pity.

She finished what she could of her salad—a lump in the throat made swallowing difficult—and shoved herself to her feet. Needing to pick up the TBA letter from Mrs. Olson gave her a good excuse to bug out early.

Nothing had ever come between her and Rhonda before. The thought of "The Jerk," as she now called the person harassing her, made her want to slam her locker. And kick it! Guy trouble, that's what it was. Guys messing up her life. First Highstreet, now The Jerk, and Jason, Rhonda's boyfriend, coming between them. She smothered the thought of her father being a guy.

She also buried Nagger's next reminder. *It isn't guys, it's you—your temper*. Who needed to hear something like that anyway? She could feel him shaking his head, just as she was shaking her own. Why did life have to be so complicated?

Complications fled when she read the letter to the

government class. Cheers, whistles, stomping feet, clapping hands—the response made her wish Bob Diego was there to enjoy it also.

"Now class." Ms. Wainwright let the excitement build and explode before stepping forward with hands raised for attention. "Okay, that's enough. They're going to send someone out from the office to find out what happened to the teacher here." The room settled down but the grins on student faces could have lit the school.

"More good news. The note I have from the office says this class gets to vote on how the money will be used." Cheers erupted again.

"You mean you didn't know about this either?" one of the kids asked.

"Nope. Best kept secret. Lets me know why Mrs. Olson kept grinning at me in staff meeting this morning. Now, how should we go about deciding what to do with the money?"

"Throw a pizza party to end all parties." The suggestion came from one of the boys in the back of the room.

"Sorry, I asked for suggestions on how to proceed, not on what to do." She motioned to a girl toward the back.

"Form a committee?" Groans met her suggestion.

"That's one way. Stacy?"

"Each of us come up with one suggestion and we all vote."

"Good." Ms. Wainwright wrote them both on the board.

"How do we know what's really needed? Like, you know, projects the school board or some teacher has thought of?"

"Good point."

"This democracy stuff is sure slow. I say let's just have a party." Snickers followed this observation.

"Just helping you understand why it takes so long to get a bill through Congress." Ms. Wainwright perched on the tall stool she kept at the front of the room. "Any other suggestions?"

"How about we make a list of people to talk to—for suggestions you know—and all of us in the class volunteer to talk to one."

"Good idea."

"And then we could vote on the best idea."

"No, then committees could research the ideas we like best so we'd have all the information." Rhonda's red hair crackled from the excitement generated.

Ms. Wainwright finished writing all the ideas on the board. "Any more suggestions?" She waited, tossing her chalk from one hand to the other. "Good, then let's look for the process here. First, what is our ultimate goal?"

"To spend the money in the best way for Prairie High." Rhonda again, nearly bouncing in her seat.

"Well put. Anyone have any additions to her statement?"

"I still think a pizza party would be easier."

By the end of the class, they'd made a list of people to talk with and all the students had volunteered to interview one and bring back a report by Friday.

Trish chewed her bottom lip. Most of the decisions would be made the next week and she would be in Kentucky. Though she'd forgotten her anger during the discussion, it all came flooding back now. All the choices she had to make, and someone was out there trying to mess up her life even more.

"Good going, Rhonda." They stepped back to keep

from bumping each other going out the door.

"Thanks." An icicle fell from the answer and crashed on the floor.

"Can I help?" Amy asked in the car going home.

Trish shook her head. "I don't know. We've never had a fight before. I said I was sorry." *What if Rhonda stays mad forever?* The thought sent Trish crashing even lower. "What would *you* do?"

"Guess I'd go over to her house after she gets home and tell her we need to talk. I've never felt waiting for something to blow over is the best way to handle it."

"Yeah, and my dad would say to pray about it first." A car horn blared behind them. Trish jumped. Her heart hit high gear before her foot could hit the gas pedal. "Same to you," she muttered. Her hands shook on the wheel.

"Pull over, Trish. Get your breath before we go on."

Trish couldn't summon enough spit in her desert throat to answer. Instead she did as ordered.

As soon as the van stopped, she dropped her head forward on her hands—hands that gripped the steering wheel as if it were a lifeline thrown in a raging sea.

A car passing broke the silence after she turned off the ignition.

Slowly but surely her heart resumed its normal pace. She could swallow around the sand and her fingers released their stranglehold on the wheel.

"Better?"

Trish nodded.

"Okay, then let's talk about how you're feeling. In our police training we are taught how to handle the kind of stress you've been experiencing. But even so, at the end of a rough time, we find someone to talk with. There are

counselors for post traumatic stress for us. We can recognize the symptoms of a body on overload. Honey,
you've got 'em all, and it's not your fault."

"I hate him."

"That's a normal emotion. Who wouldn't?"

"And I hate being mad at people and having them
mad at me."

"You bet."

Trish sucked in a deep breath and leaned her head
back against the headrest. When she let it out, she could
feel her entire body sigh. "Why is he doing this to me?"

"I wish I knew." Amy shook her head. "I just wish I
knew."

"I'm scared." Trish could barely force the confession
past her trembling lips.

"Of course. Nut cases always scare me. Give me a
good old-fashioned robbery any day. Then you can see
who and what you're up against. Trish, there's no shame
in being afraid or angry. If you ask me, you're doing a
good job of coping."

Trish shot her a raised-eyebrow look.

"Well, most of the time. And even NBA players get
time out once in a while."

"Yeah, well, I'm a far cry from an NBA star . . ."

"But you are a star, a star athlete—only in another
field—and stars, sad to say, are most often the focus of
stalkers."

"So what do I do?"

"Keep talking. Don't try to stuff your feelings and
don't think you can handle everything yourself. There's
no crime in asking for help. That's one reason police always have buddies—we work in teams. Helps keep us
sane. Besides safe."

Trish flexed her fingers and rotated her shoulders. "Thanks, Amy." She started the car and put it in gear. "You know, I almost hate going home, just in case there's something else."

"We'll get him, Trish. I promise."

Caesar wobbled to his feet and barked one yip from the front step when Trish got out of the van. "Hey, old man—no, you stay there. I'm comin'." Trish left her stuff in the van and trotted up the sidewalk. Caesar sat on his haunches, tail dusting the concrete, one yip telling her to hurry. When she hugged him, she could feel him sway. "Still mighty weak, aren't you?" She drew back from hugging him and studied his face. His pink tongue flicked out and caught her nose. "You could have stayed inside, you know." He shuffled forward, crowding as close to her as possible and resting his muzzle against her chest.

The door opened and Marge appeared, drying her hands on a dish towel. "Sandra called from Detroit. I told her you'd call as soon as you got home. How come you're late?"

Trish buried her face in Caesar's ruff. "Kinda fell apart there for a minute."

"Amy?" Marge shifted her attention to the young woman carrying Trish's gear as well as her own up the walk. "Did something else happen?"

"No, not to worry. She's a trooper. Just needed to clarify some things." Amy dropped a pat on Caesar's head and went on into the house.

Sure, nothing happened. Trish let the thoughts ramble. *My best friend isn't speaking to me, and I nearly flipped out when a car honked at me 'cause I forgot to pay attention at a stop sign. But . . .* The thoughts rambled onto a brighter road. *At least he didn't rear end me or use obscene gestures.*

"I'm okay, Mom. How long ago did she call?" Trish gave Caesar a last pat and rose to her feet. "Man, am I thirsty! We're not out of Diet Coke, are we? I drank the last one last night."

Marge shook her head. "No, I went to the grocery store. How does fried chicken sound for dinner tonight? You don't have any mounts, do you?"

Trish shook her head before diving behind the fridge door. She popped the top on a Diet Coke can and chugged several swallows. Amazing how panic made one thirsty. But she surely wasn't going to tell her mother that bit of information.

Trish dialed the phone number in front of her, the phone tucked between shoulder and ear so she could sip from her drink at the same time. Hard to believe she was really going to be in an ad for one of the big three American car companies.

"I have some news I think you'll find exciting," Sandra said after the greetings. "Are you sitting down?"

"No, but I will." Trish pushed herself up on the counter. "Okay, what?" She listened intently. "Really! You're kidding."

CHAPTER TEN

"Red's going to be in the ads too? You're not just making this up?" Trish slapped her free hand on the counter. "I can't believe it. He doesn't know any more about acting than I do."

"The lines won't be difficult, we promise."

"Lines—I forgot about lines."

"Don't worry, Trish, you're going to have a ball with this."

Amy and Marge stood in front of Trish, hands on hips, waiting for some answers. Trish waved them back with her free hand. She didn't dare release her clutch on the phone. If she did, this crazy dream might just spin away.

She listened while Sandra gave her more instructions. Their tickets were all booked and would arrive by overnight express. All she needed for the shoot were several sets of silks, her helmet, and all the other gear she used every day. Trish nodded her understanding, then caught herself. These weren't video phones, not yet, so she added "uh-huh's" in all the right places. When she finally hung up the phone, she leaped to the floor.

113

Arms in the air, she did an Indian dance, first around Amy, then Marge. "You won't believe all what's happening."

"It would help if you'd tell us." Marge leaned back against the counter. "I'm sorry it's such bad news."

"Yeah, terrible. Trish." Amy grabbed the dancer's arm. "Tell me, now!"

"Red's going to be in the commercials with Spitfire and me."

"Got that part."

"We leave Sunday morning."

"Okay."

"They're sending three tickets. One for you." Trish tapped her finger on Amy's chest. "You ever been to Kentucky, m'dear?"

Amy looked as if someone had doused the sun. "No, and I'd love to go, but the department isn't planning on sending me."

Trish danced again. "They don't have to. Chrysler wants you along to protect me, and they'll pay you and your expenses. If Parks won't let—"

"It isn't his decision. It's the chief's."

"Don't worry. Sandra is taking care of that too. You have vacation time coming—use it for this, or else she said something about a loan. You know, like an interlibrary loan. Only you're not a book." Trish quit dancing to double over with laughter at her joke.

Amy and Marge laughed along with her. Who could resist?

"Maybe I'll really get to go?" Amy copied Trish's thumping dance step. "Who-ee."

"Just call Sandra a miracle worker. Come on, Mom, get in the act." She pulled her mother into the chorus line. "We're going to Kentucky on Sunday." She stopped so fast, Amy bumped into her. "We're flying first-class." She whooped again. "I gotta call Rhonda. Wait 'til she hears this."

At the thought, her dancing feet planted themselves firmly on the floor. *What if Rhonda still won't talk to me?*

"What is it, Tee?" Marge leaned back against the counter. When Trish told her the sorry tale, she shook her head. "All these years you two got along so well, and now, wouldn't you know, a guy comes between you."

"It's all my fault."

"Well, I've learned through the years that it takes two to fight but only one to begin the making up. You've got a couple of horses who need training, and then I suggest you go see Rhonda. That way she can't hang up on you."

"You're right." Trish stared out the window. "Isn't Brad coming over?"

"Not today. He had something else he had to do. I'll help you."

"Me too. That way I can loosen up these aching muscles from riding yesterday. And I thought I was in good shape." Amy rubbed her inner thighs. "I better call the chief too—find out what he thinks about my trip to Kentucky. How long we gonna be there?" She chuckled, her voice carrying a sinister tone. "Wait 'til Parks hears about this."

As soon as the horses were all brushed and fed, Trish turned to leave Amy at the house and jog down the long drive.

"Where you going?" Amy stopped her with a hand on her arm.

"Over to Rhonda's. Why?"

"Not by yourself you're not."

"Amy, it's just down the road, not even half a mile away."

"We'll drive and I'll wait in the car." Amy snagged the van keys off the hook above the phone. "Come on."

Trish gave her a disgusted look but did as told. The phone rang just as they closed the front door behind them.

"Hang on." Amy tossed Trish the keys.

Trish watched the symptoms strike her body. Speeding heart, tight stomach, clenched fists. Even her hair seemed to lift from her neck. All because of the ringing phone. Sure, she was handling all of this just fine.

"It's for you. They're ready to release your car."

Trish took the offered receiver. "But I can't pick it up tomorrow. I have to be at the track right after school," she said after listening to the caller. "How about later in the evening?" She groaned at his answer. "Just a minute." She put her hand over the receiver so she could listen to Amy.

"You can have the repair shop pick your car up if you know who's going to do the bodywork."

Trish nodded her thanks and gave the instructions to the caller. When she hung up, she reached for the phone book. "You sure make my life easier," she told Amy. "You want to take on the job of big sister permanently?"

"Well, if I had my choice, I couldn't find a better baby sister anywhere." Amy gave Trish a quick one-arm hug.

Blurry eyes made it hard for Trish to decipher the phone number of the body shop. They'd be able to pick up her car, no problem, and a paint repair like that would take two weeks. Trish groaned. They'd call with the estimate as soon as they saw the damage. She hung up the phone, shaking her head. "Everything takes so long."

"You don't want them to rush a paint job like this. They gonna touch it up or repaint the entire vehicle?"

"They'll let me know when they see it." Trish shuddered at the memory. "I'm glad I don't have to see it again before it's finished." Together they headed for the van and Rhonda's house.

"Sorry, Trish, she's not home yet," Mrs. Seaboldt answered when Trish stuck her head in the door. "Jason is taking her out to dinner and an early movie."

"On Wednesday?"

"I know, there go the rules, but you kids are seniors now. Guess you should be able to make your own decisions—right?"

"Yeah, I guess. Ummm—don't tell her I was here, okay?"

"Trish, is there a problem?" Tall and with hair several shades darker than Rhonda's carrot top, Mrs. Seaboldt came to the door. She studied Trish through emerald eyes of love. "Okay, my other daughter, what's up?"

"Nothing much." Trish couldn't look her in the face. "I'll get back to her later." She turned and waved over her shoulder. "See ya."

"Kinda reminds me of a stakeout," Amy said when Jason's car had finally left the Seaboldt home a bit after nine. This was her and Trish's third drive by. "As I said, I'll wait out here."

With her thumb cuticles chewed raw and her bottom lip feeling like it might begin to bleed any moment, Trish sucked in a life-giving breath when she mounted the stairs to the back door. All these years of running back and forth and nearly living at each other's houses, here she was having a terrible time going in.

"Please, God," she muttered the words she'd been praying all evening. "Please make Rhonda listen to me and forgive me. I can't stand having her mad at me." When she entered the Dutch blue kitchen, Mrs. Seaboldt pointed upstairs. Trish heard Rhonda's voice on the phone.

"Thanks, Mom. Tell her I'll call later or she can call me when she gets home."

Trish felt her heart leap right up into her throat. Rhonda had been trying to call *her*.

"This soon enough?" Trish stepped through the door into Rhonda's teal and mauve room.

"Trish, I . . ."

Trish held up her hand, traffic-cop style. "Me first. I've been practicing all evening. Please forgive me for being such a downer and for my mean remarks about Jason. I'm really sorry."

"No, it was my fault. I know all the terrible stuff that's been going on. I shoulda been more understanding."

The two friends collided midway between the bed and the door. Between hugs and giggles, along with a bit of cheek wiping, they made their forgiveness definite. They both flopped backward on the bed.

"Man, let's don't ever do this again." Trish laid the back of her hand across her forehead. "I can't take it."

"Me neither." Silence but for their breathing rested gently on them.

"How was the movie?" Trish elbowed Rhonda in the ribs.

"Funny." Her voice settled into dreamy. "Trish, he's

such a neat guy—not a kid like all the boys we know."

"Is he a good kisser?"

"Tricia Marie Evanston!" Rhonda picked up a pillow and bopped her friend in the face. "That's none of your business."

Trish rolled over on her stomach, feet in the air. "Well, is he?"

"How should I know? He's the first guy I've really kissed." Rhonda assumed the stomach position also and crammed the pillow under her chin. The silence draped comfortably around the room.

"So, what's gone on today in the saga of Trish Evanston, girl jockey?"

"Well, we haven't heard from what's-his-name."

"The Jerk!"

"But . . ." and Trish went on to tell Rhonda all about the phone calls. "So, Red and I'll be on national television." She finished her tale. "Awesome, huh?" She turned her head. "Oh my gosh, Amy's out in the van." She bounded to her feet. "What a creep I am!" The two girls pounded down the stairs to find Amy sitting in the kitchen sharing a cup of coffee with Mrs. Seaboldt. "I forgot you."

"No foolin'. But don't worry, this bodyguard knows how to take care of herself. You ready to go home now?" She glanced at her watch. "It's after ten."

Once in the car, Amy only asked, "How did it go?"

"She was calling *me*," Trish laughed.

"Good. I like happy endings."

Trish's last thought before dropping into the canyon of sleep was about Red. She'd forgotten to call him in all the uproar. *Tomorrow*, she promised herself. *I'll call him tomorrow.*

But Thursday passed in such a blur, Trish managed to forget several things, including calling Red. With a win and two places at the track, she felt pretty good, and when there'd been no contact from The Jerk, she felt even better.

She groaned when she heard the clock strike nine. Kentucky was two hours ahead so Red was already sound asleep. She'd be seeing him before she'd have a chance to talk with him.

"You got a minute?" Amy paused in the door of Trish's bedroom.

"Sure."

"Want to hear some good news?" Amy settled down on the bed. At Trish's nod, she continued. "I talked with the chief."

"And?" Trish prodded her to hurry.

"And I get to go!" Amy pummeled the pillow she'd nestled in her lap. "I'm going to Kentucky! And it's on someone else's dime."

Trish applauded her friend's excitement. "What does Kevin think about it?"

"My loving and extremely understanding fiancé says to have a great time. Says he's pea green with jealousy, but I'm not to pay any attention to that, just go and take care of you." Amy grinned at Trish, leaning back in her chair with her hands locked behind her head. The blonde nodded and her eyes grew dreamy. "He's a pretty special guy, that man of mine."

"I'm glad. Both 'cause you're coming and 'cause he's so special. When do I get to meet him?"

"Probably when you—we—get home." Amy returned the pillow to its rightful place. "He's still in L.A. teaching at the Academy. These long-distance relationships are the pits."

"You're telling me," Trish agreed, thinking again of the phone call that never was.

Trish awoke feeling sure she'd run a hundred miles during the nightmare. Who was it that kept chasing her all night but managed to keep his face hidden? Or did he have a face? She lay in bed, trying to remember. You'd think by now she'd have recognized him anywhere, she'd looked over her shoulder so many times to see him about to grab her.

Just thinking about it set her heart to thundering again. She swung her feet to the floor and staggered down the hall. Feeling run over by a truck was getting to be a habit.

She jumped when her mother knocked on the door to remind her she'd better hurry. A car horn set her pulses to pounding. A slamming locker slammed her heart against her ribs. Even at the track, she kept wanting to look over her shoulder. She hurried from the women's dressing room out to the saddling paddock. Today for sure she didn't want to dwell on the sound of shots echoing in the cavernous building. But she'd heard them and she hadn't forgotten the sound.

"What's happenin', lass?" Patrick laid a hand on her knee after giving her a boost into the saddle.

Trish stared down into his faded blue eyes, surrounded by the crinkles of a man used to the out-of-doors. "Just more of the same—nightmares—can't forget what went on here."

"Well, now, you concentrate on that filly 'neath you and the race ahead. Let Amy worry about lookin' out for you. 'Tis her job, that's what." He patted her knee again.

"And I'll be prayin' extra guardian angels round about you besides." He winked at her. "And ye'll be knowin' nothing gets through them."

"You're right." She stroked her hand down the filly's bright sorrel shoulder. "Come on, girl. Let's just give it the best we've got." When they trotted out beside the pony rider, Trish lifted her face to the breeze coming off the river. On around the track, she could see the sliding sun painting the cloud strata with a lavish brush of reds and oranges, tinged with purple and gold. The filly snorted and tossed her head, setting her mane to bouncing and Trish to chuckling.

"You're ready, you are." Her voice took on its cadence of comfort, gentling both herself and the filly she rode.

Since she'd come in fifth in the last race, Trish settled into the saddle, determined to win. The filly she rode had missed a win by only a nose her first time out, so winning wasn't a pipe dream. "Please God, take good care of us." Her murmured prayer fit into the song she'd been crooning up 'til then.

The filly burst out of the gate and hit her stride as if she'd been running for years. Trish let two duelers take the lead coming out of the first turn and hung off the pace only a length. Down the backstretch she held her place, the filly seeming content to obey her rider. With two furlongs to go, Trish loosened the reins and commanded the filly to fly.

With powerful strides she did just that. They blew by the remaining leader as if the horse had quit, still picking up speed when they crossed the finish line.

"And that's number three, Money Ahead, owned by John Anderson and ridden by Trish Evanston, winner by two lengths." The announcement crackled over the speaker.

"Way to go." Genie Stokes cantered beside Trish as they rounded the turn back to the grandstand. "You have any idea she'd be that fast?"

"No, Anderson raced her in Minnesota because we weren't sure about opening here. Patrick took over a month ago." Trish brought her down to a trot. "She sure can run."

"Told you to just concentrate." Patrick beamed up at her when he took the rein to lead them into the winner's circle.

"Did you think she'd be that fast?" Trish leaned forward to speak for Patrick's ears only.

"I'd hoped so. John seems pretty set on her."

"Excellent ride, Trish." Anderson greeted her with a broad grin. "Pretty nice, isn't she?" He rubbed the filly's nose. "And look, I don't have to worry about being bitten."

They posed for the picture and Trish leaped lightly to the ground. "Not like our friend Gatesby, huh?"

"Friend, right." Anderson shook hands with a fan. "Thanks, yes, we're thinking of running her at a mile." He turned back to Trish. "If there were only some way of breaking that monster."

"We tried. Gatesby just thinks it's a game and he likes to win." Trish stepped back off the scale. "You bought yourself a winner there. See ya." She headed back toward the women's jockey room, Amy falling in beside her.

"Trish, could you sign my program?" The question came from both sides of the walk. Trish smiled, joked with her fans and signed programs. She turned to leave when a deep voice drew her back.

"How about signing my program?"

Trish looked up into the bluest eyes she'd ever seen. Smiling, fringed with sooty black lashes, the kind of eyes girls die for and guys get—total unfairness in the distribution of features. His smile bordered on the punch-in-the-solar-plexus type.

"Sh-sure." Trish caught her lip between her teeth. Since when did smiles become so contagious? "There you go. Thanks for coming today."

"Oh, you'll see me again, you can count on it."

Trish felt a little shiver at his words. Who was he?

CHAPTER ELEVEN

"Who was that?" Amy sounded like Trish felt. Out of breath.

"Got me, but if Rhonda'd been here, she'd have fainted dead away. What a gorgeous guy!"

"That's putting it mildly. I wonder if the talent scouts from Hollywood have seen him?"

"Amy, you're engaged, remember?"

"You bet I do, sweetie, but there's no law against lookin' and he's definitely worth looking at." She pushed open the door to the dressing room and held it for Trish. "You have any idea who he is?"

"Never saw him before in my life and probably won't again." Trish tossed her helmet down on the bench. "Did you see that filly take off? What I wouldn't give for three of her in my string." Trish shucked her silks and pulled off her boots. She had two races before she'd be up again. While yakking with the other jockeys was always fun, she pulled out her government textbook. The week she returned from Kentucky she'd have some big tests, and there wouldn't be much time to study once she got to Kentucky.

She finished the day with a place and headed out to the parking lot for her car. Most of the fans had gone home, leaving the cleaning crew to sweep up the debris. Sounds echoed in the concrete hall. Trish shivered. Sounds, including shots, still echoed in her head.

"You as hungry as I am?" Amy asked from right beside her shoulder. Trish flinched. "Okay, what's happening?" Amy could switch from friend to protector within the blink of an eye.

"Just remembering. I hate this feeling of wanting to look over my shoulder all the time and being afraid to."

"Don't blame you. All I can say is it will eventually go away. Just takes time." Amy scanned the parking lot. "Trish, anyone would feel the way you do with what you've been through. I know I sound like a broken record, but don't be so hard on yourself."

"Now you sound like my dad." Trish unlocked the van door and swung her bags in.

"I take that as a compliment. From all I hear and see, that man was one wise fellow. Makes me wish I'd had someone like him in my life." She fastened her seat belt. "Let's get outa here. I could eat a—whoops, guess I won't say that anymore. Cow—that's right. I could eat a cow."

"Burgers okay?"

"Nuh-uh. I want real food. Steak, baked potato, Caesar salad, the works. Or will your mom have dinner ready?"

"She always has something I can warm up, but she knows I usually stop on the way home. Too hungry to wait."

"Good then, we'll start with an appetizer that's quick. Lead me to it."

After a dinner that left them both stuffed to the gills,

Trish felt only like falling into bed when they finally got home. She glared at the stack of books on her desk, promised them time the next day, and hit the sack. Her three praises—"Thank you for keeping me and all of us safe today, thank you for the win on the filly, thank you for Amy"—left her asleep before the amen.

Morning dawned cold, wet, and windy, but by the time silver cracked the eastern horizon, Trish had already taken two mounts on their designated trips around the track. While her slicker kept out the worst, both wet and cold slipped down the back of her neck. When she dismounted at the barns, she clapped her arms around her chest a couple of times and tucked her hands into her armpits.

"Man, I'm gonna race in California or Florida next year. This is the pits." She stamped her feet to get the circulation moving. "I think my nose is froze clear off."

"Can't be." Brad led up her next mount. "It's still running."

"Thank you so very much, Mr. Observant. You got any other words of wisdom for me?"

"No, but I'll buy breakfast soon as we're done. Having Amy here speeds things up, so we can get warmed up faster."

Trish waved to the blonde scraping down the last horse she'd ridden. "Don't you wish you'd stayed home in bed?"

Amy shot her a dirty look.

Trish waved again and raised her knee into Brad's waiting cupped hands. Once mounted, she pulled her neck down into her shoulders, turtle style. "See you guys. You might make me a cup of hot chocolate while I'm gone, Brad. Your coffee's strong enough to knock Gatesby here over."

The gelding tossed his head and jigged to the side at the sound of his name. "You don't like the miserable weather either, do you?" Trish patted his neck and smoothed a lock of mane to the right side. "Well, let's get it over with so we can both go back to the barn. You at least get a nice warm stall—I get more horses to ride."

———

By race time the clouds hung low, but the rain had ceased. Trish glared up at the glass-fronted stands. For sure there'd be no racing if the fans had to brave the weather like the entertainment did.

Everyone out took the first turn cautiously. No matter how hard the maintenance crew worked, today the track would be muddy. Trish thanked the Lord above that she rode a mudder. Her mount didn't care what the weather was like; in fact, the wetter the better. He didn't mind mud in his face, but he'd rather be in front slinging it.

Trish let him take the lead, holding him back so that he wouldn't wear out. "Think you're part mule, old man," she sang to his twitching ears. "You'd probably run straight up a mountain." He won by two lengths.

When Trish met Bob Diego in front of the grandstand, he nodded his approval from under a wide-brimmed western hat. "You rode that just right, mi amiga. Congratulations."

"Thanks." Trish smiled for the camera and baled off. "See you for the eighth." She picked up her sidekick and trotted back to the locker room. "Thank God for showers." She stood under the driving water for ten minutes before she felt warm enough to leave.

Back up in the third, the overcast had deteriorated to a mist. Patrick gave her a leg up, along with a reminder. "Be careful out there. Coming back in one piece is more important than winning."

"You're not telling me anything new. I hate weather like this." Her mount shook his head. "And he does too." The call of the bugle floated back into the dim, spoke-wheeled saddling paddock. "Pray us some angels. We may need them."

Trish wished more people would train their horses decently, or scratch those who hated the rain, when it took three tries to get one stubborn creature into the starting gates. His whinny of alarm set everyone's teeth on edge, not helped by the rain now drifting in sheets across the track.

She breathed a prayer of relief when everyone made it around the first turn with only a couple of minor slips. Down the backstretch, she kept her mount to the outside, off the pace by a length. Going into the turn, the two jockeys on either side of her made their moves. She heard the slap of the bats over the grunts of horses giving their best and the pounding hooves.

The horse on the inside slipped, caromed off the rail, and banged the animal beside Trish. Like dominoes, the force sent her mount staggering for footing, slipping and slopping in the treacherous mud.

Trish clung with all her might, her arms taut like steel bands, trying to keep her horse on his feet. Her heart thundered like the horses behind. An animal screamed. A jockey yelled.

But Trish had her horse straightened out again and

running free. She shot a glance over her shoulder. Two down at least, other back runners pulling wide to keep from injuring either themselves or those down. By the time they reached the finish line, her mount was favoring his left foreleg.

"Thank God you kept him to the outside like you did or you'da been right there in the middle." Patrick took the gelding's reins and shook his head. "My heart was in me mouth, that it was."

"How bad was it?"

"I don't think too bad. Both horses got up again and the jockeys were up and walking." Brad bent down to check out the gelding's foreleg. "This guy's gonna need some ice."

"Looks like those guardian angels you prayed for had their hands full back there." Trish dismounted to ease the weight on her horse. "Do you know who went down?"

"Genie was one and a young apprentice the other. He shoulda knowed better than pushin' at that point." Patrick shook his head. "These young pups put too much on winnin' and not enough on giving their horse a good ride."

"That was too close." Amy fell in beside Trish after she stepped off the scale.

"You won't catch me arguing with that." Trish shivered. "I'm freezing."

Genie Stokes was already in the shower when Trish got back to the dressing room. "You okay?" Trish called above the water's rush.

"I will be. One good thing about mud—it helps cushion your fall." She turned off the taps and poked her head out the curtain. "I could smack that kid right up alongside the head though. What a stupid move."

"They gonna file a grievance?"

"Doubt it. 'Bout the time I calm down, I'm gonna give him a grievance or two."

"I'm just glad you're not hurt."

"Yeah, then you'd have to get your sorry butt over here in the mornings and work your own horses." She disappeared back behind the curtain.

"Right." Trish rejoined Amy on the bench and pulled off her boots. She felt like a major mud blob herself, and she'd stayed on top of her horse.

She only managed a show on Diego's horse in the feature race of the day. "Sorry."

"No problem. I almost scratched her myself. She doesn't like the mud too well."

"Horses around here should get used to it."

"They say mudpacks are good for the complexion, no?" Diego tipped the brim of his hat.

"Gracias, amigo. I'll keep that in mind." Trish turned to head for the showers. "See you in Kentucky."

Trish signed a couple of programs and thanked her fans for coming, all the while trying to keep a smile on her face and the shivers from ruining her signature. She'd just turned to leave when a deep voice stopped her.

"If you don't mind?" The gorgeous guy from the day before took up more than his share of space on the other side of the fence. In the gloom his shoulders looked broader than a football player's. And his eyes—those incredible eyes.

"Who should I make it to?" Trish couldn't resist smiling back.

"No matter, your autograph is enough." His voice—what could one call it but sexy?

Trish signed the program with a flourish and handed it back to him. "Thanks for coming, in spite of the weather."

He took the program back and touched it to his forehead before walking away.

"You care to put your police powers to work to find out who he is?" Trish stared after the cashmere-jacket-clad back.

"I thought you liked Red."

"I do, but . . ."

"I know, he's dynamite." The two headed for the locker room, laughing at themselves and each other.

Since Trish was finished for the day, she showered again and picked up her bag. "You know, I can get used to having a valet. Thanks for packing my stuff."

"At your service. Just means we can get home faster and crank up that fireplace. Your mom said she invited company for dinner."

"Who?"

Amy shrugged. "Got me."

Company included Brad, Rhonda, and Patrick.

"I decided we needed a send-off dinner." Marge set the platter of fried chicken on the table. "After all, it's not everyday my daughter turns from jockey to model and then rides in the Breeder's Cup. And our Spitfire stars in the same commercial." She set the mashed potatoes and gravy in place.

Amy brought the broccoli and cheese and a basket of fluffy biscuits.

"Mrs. E, you sure know the way to this man's stomach." Brad took his place at the end of the table, where David usually sat.

"Man? What man?" Trish looked around the room

and even under the table. "The only man I see here is Patrick." She turned to Amy. "What about you?"

Amy shook her head. "I'm staying out of this one." She took the chair next to Rhonda. "What about you?"

"Just feed me. I've been studying all day."

"Poor baby, in a nice warm room, dry, no wind. My heart bleeds for you."

"Yeah, and how much did you earn today?"

"Enough, children. Let's eat." Marge raised both hands, traffic-cop style. "Trish, you say the blessing."

The teasing continued on through dinner and into an evening in front of the fireplace. When Brad took out the black mesh popcorn popper, Amy flopped back on the floor with a groan.

"I didn't know people really did this anymore. In my book, popcorn is a microwave miracle."

"Wait 'til you taste it." Trish handed Brad a mitten-style hot pad. The fragrance of popping corn floated through the room, teasing nostrils and taste buds. "Shake harder, big B, so you don't burn it."

"You do it, smarty." He handed her the wooden handle. "I'll get a bowl." Bounding to his feet, Brad headed for the kitchen. As he went by, the phone rang, so he reached over and picked it up.

"No, Brad." Amy leaped to her feet.

"Runnin' On Farm. Hello? Hel—lo." He held the phone away from his ear. "Funny, I could have sworn someone was listening." He dropped the receiver back in the cradle just as Amy reached him. "Wrong number, I guess."

"Brad, I'm the one who answers all the calls here. Now, did the person say anything?"

Brad shook his head.

"Did you hear any background noise?"

Again, a head shake. "Sorry, Amy. It was just such a habit. Phone rings, whoever's closest picks it up."

"I know. Tell me exactly what you heard."

Brad scrunched his brows to think better. He shook his head again. "Nothing, no sound at all. I didn't wait for a click, so they might have already hung up."

Trish wrapped her arms around her raised knees. Maybe this was nothing at all—and then again—maybe not.

Chapter Twelve

"Well, I for one am glad Amy's going with you."
Rhonda sat cross-legged in the middle of Trish's bed.

"I can tell. I mean if Chrysler wants to pay her way
that's fine with me, but me needing a bodyguard, that's
a bit ridiculous."

Rhonda's eyebrows arched right into her flyaway
bangs.

"I mean anywhere but here." Trish, mirroring Rhonda's pose, leaned forward and rested her forehead on the
pillow she clutched in her somewhat lap. "Rhonda, this
whole thing is absolutely insane." The pillow muffled
her voice.

"I know. Tee, I keep praying all the time that God will
keep you safe. You're my best friend—we're more like
sisters, you know." Rhonda smoothed a hand down the
back of Trish's head. "And if it takes a bodyguard to keep
you safe until The Jerk is caught, I'd pay for one myself."

Trish could hear the tears hovering just behind
Rhonda's words. She groped for Rhonda's hand.
"Thanks, buddy." A moment of silence stretched to the
end of the clock chiming midnight. Trish sat up straight.
"Guess that tells us something."

"What?" Rhonda swiped a drop of moisture from one eye.

"Bedtime." Trish bonked her friend on the head with the pillow. "I have a plane to catch at seven-fifty, as in A.M."

"Tell me about it. I'm the designated driver, remember?"

"Thanks, buddy," Trish murmured after they were both snugged under their covers.

"For what?" Rhonda's voice said she was already half-asleep.

"For everything."

"You're welcome."

Two of Trish's many praises that night included Rhonda. Just think, by tomorrow evening she would be seeing Spitfire. She wrapped both arms around her pillow and hugged it. *I'm comin', fella, I'm comin'.*

They couldn't have asked for a better flight. Greeting the Shipsons felt like coming home to Trish. *How lucky I am,* she thought, waiting by the luggage carousel. *I have three homes. Washington, California, and Kentucky. And a mother at each one.* She glanced over at Bernice Shipson chatting away with Marge as if they'd been friends forever.

"Your friend is anxious to see you." Donald Shipson told her as he swung luggage up onto an airport cart. "Timmy says all he does is mention your name and Spitfire looks around to see where you are. He's one smart horse, that one."

"Have you talked with Adam yet?"

"Oh, sure. Saw him day before yesterday when I had

a horse running at the Downs. He says your Firefly has a good chance if all goes well."

"Sounds like Adam all right. I can't wait to ride there again. There's just something about Churchill Downs."

"I agree. And while the Derby is tops, I'd rather race there anytime of the season, even more than Keeneland. By the way, you're not excited about the Chrysler deal or anything, are you?"

"Oh, not a bit. How about you?"

"Oh, I—we have commercials filmed at BlueMist every other week, didn't you know?" He winked at her as he beckoned to the women. "Bernice is heading for orbit any time now. And Sarah's been baking for a week. Red said to tell you he'll see you first thing in the morning."

"He's been doing real well, hasn't he?"

"You're talkin' about that fine young jockey who's been bringing our horses into the money nearly every time?" Bernice locked her arm through Trish's. "Mr. Shipson's had you to himself just long enough. Now it's my turn." She took Amy's arm on the other side. "Sarah—that's our cook—is so happy to have young people to fuss over . . . and the filming crew. Why, she's in her glory."

"I think I've died and gone to heaven," Amy whispered when she followed Trish into the plush rear seat of the silver Cadillac.

"Wait 'til you see BlueMist. Just like Scarlett O'Hara could step out the front door herself."

"You a *Gone with the Wind* fan too?"

"Read the book even before I saw the movie."

Donald Shipson pointed the landmarks out to Amy while they drove around the city of Lexington and out to BlueMist Farms. Amy reminded Trish of herself the first time she'd been taken on this route—all eyes and ears.

Now with a different season, the views had changed again. All the oaks and maples had left their green dresses and now danced in hues of rust and gold and vermilion. Horses raced across the paddocks, trying to outrun the breeze and snorting when stopped by the wooden fences.

"I thought all the board fences were painted white back here, but I see equal numbers of black."

"Owners found it cheaper for upkeep, and they still looked mighty fine, so that's a trend. The purist who can afford it stays with the white, and I have to admit, I like white best."

"That's because he doesn't have to do the painting." Bernice turned to look over her shoulder. "You've never been to Kentucky before, Amy?" Bernice gave her a wink. "Well, we'll just have to make sure y'all see as much as you can. Just so's you'll want to come back. Our house is yours any time you can visit again."

"She means it too," Trish whispered near Amy's ear. "You'll leave here so spoiled you can't wait to get back."

Trish could hardly sit still any longer, when they finally turned into the long curving drive of BlueMist Farms. All the trees that lined the asphalt road had joined the fall finery parade. Trish sucked in her breath and exhaled pure delight. "Wow. I've never seen anything like this."

Marge sighed with pleasure. "It's been so long since I've seen midwest fall color I'd almost forgotten how stunning it can be. But then I expect the vistas you have here are beautiful any season."

Trish could see the stallion barn over the creek and off to the left. Spitfire waited for her. She gave a bounce of excitement on the seat. It seemed like years instead of weeks since she'd hugged her big black colt.

Before the car finished moving, she had her door open and sent her whistle slicing through the air. A trumpet call answered her and then another. Other stallions answered the strident whinny until it sounded like an equestrian chorus in C major.

Trish started running before her feet touched the ground. Or maybe they never did. She whistled again— high, low, high—and jerked open the Dutch door to the cedar-paneled stallion barn.

She bit back the tears when she saw Spitfire, his chest tight against the webbing gate, straining to reach her with his muzzle extended to the limit.

"Hey, fella, looks like you missed me about as much as I did you." She threw her arms around his neck with a hug to end all hugs, then rubbed his ears and under the heavy mane. "I think you get more beautiful all the time. You look like a grown-up horse now, not just a colt." Spitfire snuffled her hair and lipped her cheek, all the while his nostrils quivering in a soundless nicker.

"Trish, he's incredible." Amy stopped a few feet back and shook her head. "I mean, I knew he was something from his pictures, but what a horse!"

"He is kinda special, isn't he?" Trish turned and Spitfire draped his head over her shoulder, just as if she'd never been away.

"He knew you were coming." Timmy O'Ryan, Spitfire's personal groom, joined the group. "All I have to do is mention your name and he looks all around for you."

"He's my buddy." Trish smoothed the long black forelock and down Spitfire's nose. "Aren'tcha, fella?" Spitfire closed his eyes and sighed, bliss evident in every muscle and bone of his body.

"Going to be interesting to see what kind of colts he throws. If they're anything like him, there'll be some mighty happy owners."

"Yeah, wish I had more mares to send to him." Trish motioned to Amy. "Come on over here and meet my friend. He likes blondes."

"Just be glad you aren't wearing a hat." Timmy touched the brim of his tan porkpie cap.

"Why, what would happen?" Amy stepped up beside Trish. "Gosh, he's huge."

"Yeah, they're letting you get fat, aren't they, fella? You couldn't race now if your life depended on it."

"There's a difference between breeding fitness and racing, all right. But his stamina's still right up there. He'll come back from galloping a couple of times around the track without even blowing." Timmy stopped just out of Spitfire's reach. "I warned all those photographer folks. I think they think I'm kidding."

Trish laid her cheek against Spitfire's. "You'll show them, won't you?" He nodded without lifting his head.

Amy stroked the opposite side of his neck. "So he not only understands English, he talks too?"

"Sarah has supper ready." Bernice returned from making a call at the wall phone by the door. "Think you can pull yourself away long enough to eat?"

"She'd bring him with her if you let her," Marge teased.

"I'll be back." Trish dropped a kiss on the black's nose and eased away. Immediately his whinny echoed and reechoed in the high-ceilinged room. "You be good." He leaned forward as if to go right through the gate.

"I'll stay with him." Timmy stepped forward and, with a hand on Spitfire's muzzle, eased him backward before the gate came off its hinges.

Trish followed the others out the door with a last long look over her shoulder. "I'll be back, I promise." She could hear his pleading whinnies long after the car pulled away, for when they faded from her ears she could still hear them with her heart.

"Oh, my." Amy clutched Trish's arm. "Y'all weren't just a whistlin' Dixie were you, sugar?" Amy whispered her southern drawl in Trish's ear. She'd just had her first glimpse of the big house at BlueMist.

"Wait 'til Bernice takes you around. I learned more history in an hour with her than in a year at school." Trish slid out of the car. "And it was a whole lot more fun too." She tried to hide her giggles when Amy followed the Shipsons up the wide steps to the fan-lit front door. Three tall white pillars graced the edge of the veranda on either side of them. Three wicker rocking chairs with floral cushions visited in front of the parlor French doors.

Amy wore the same star-struck expression Trish knew she'd adopted the first time she visited. BlueMist did that to guests.

"Aren't you glad you got voted to be my bodyguard?" Trish asked.

They'd dropped Amy's bags off in her room and now stood in front of the tall casement windows of Trish's room, looking out over the rose garden.

"I know I was meant to have a life-style like this, but that bloomin' stork who delivered me went to the wrong address." Amy turned and looked around the room with its rose-patterned rugs and canopied four-poster bed. "I feel so young with all these old, old pieces being used like everyday furniture. This could all be in a museum."

"We better get downstairs. Sarah likes everyone there when she brings the food in. I'm warning you, she'll try to make sure you gain ten pounds. Says we're all too skinny."

Together they descended the walnut staircase. "And you know what?" Trish went on. "The Shipsons are such real people."

When they left the table they were all groaning, just as Trish had warned. After a jog down to the barn to say good-night to Spitfire, they joined the rest of the group in the parlor.

"Trish, Amy, I'd like you to meet Joseph Silverstein, Artistic Director for Merritt Advertising Agency. He'll be producing the commercials. You can say he runs the show."

"I'm pleased to meet you." Trish felt a quiver down in her middle, maybe because a whip-lean man who looked like he'd stepped out of the pages of *Gentleman's Quarterly*, a high-class fashion magazine, was studying her as if she were a bug under a microscope.

"Likewise." His concentration never wavered. "Unbraid your hair please."

"What?"

"Your hair. Let it loose." Trish raised trembling fingers and did as he asked. "There, that's better. Hair with riches like yours shouldn't be bound. We'll shoot you with it down."

"But I don't wear it that way when I have my helmet on."

"So, no helmet."

Trish felt the quiver turn to flame. Who did this guy think he was? Hadn't he done *any* research on horse racing?

"But when I'm riding I have to wear the helmet."

"We'll see." He walked around her, one finger tapping his chin.

The bug under the microscope began to squirm. Trish shot Donald a look of pleading, but all she got back was a shrug. She straightened her spine and returned look for look. *Shape up,* she ordered herself when she felt her teeth start to bite her bottom lip. She raised her chin a mite farther.

When he finally smiled, she caught herself just before letting out a whoosh of air. She smiled back, a right eyebrow slightly raised, in a barely-uncovering-her-teeth smile.

"That's it. Give me that look on camera tomorrow and we'll wind this up way ahead of schedule." A blow to the solar plexus wouldn't have winded Trish more.

It was as if no one else in the room had breathed before then either. A community whoosh made everyone smile, and when the conversation picked up, they all talked just a bit louder and brighter.

What kind of power does this guy have? Trish let herself study him now that he was talking with Donald. *I may be only seventeen, but even I recognize power when I see it. Is the whole shoot going to be this nerve-wracking?* But while she could come up with plenty of questions, she didn't dare ask them. Who wanted to be that bug under the scope anyway?

––––––––––

As they'd announced, Sarah started serving breakfast at five-thirty. The hubbub from the dining room made Trish hurry to get showered and dressed. She met Amy in the hall and they descended the stairs together.

"You'll keep them from eating me, won't you?" Trish asked halfway down.

"You made it through the inquisition last night. You don't need me." Amy, one step behind, laid a hand on Trish's shoulder. "But I'll be there. Count on it. Besides, I wouldn't miss this for anything."

The hand on Trish's shoulder spread comfort through her entire body.

"Okay, folks, we've got a bad weather report, so we'll get the running shots while it's still nice out. That early morning haze'll be in about an hour, so hustle."

A young woman with her straight hair pulled back in two clips stopped at Trish's chair. "Hi, I'm Meg. Here's your script for today's shoot." She checked her watch. "You need to be down at wardrobe in forty-five minutes."

"But I'm already wearing everything but my silks."

"Makeup's there too. You better move it."

Trish stuffed the last of her biscuit in her mouth and pushed back her chair. "Come on, Amy. Duty calls."

Shipson drove them down to a parking lot now full of trailers, cars, and trucks with people striding purposefully between them, all seeming to know exactly what they were doing. "That's wardrobe . . . makeup over there. Red won't be here 'til later since at this point the shoots with him are scheduled for tomorrow."

"Thanks, I was wondering." Trish beat back the urge to hide under the dash and instead nudged Amy to get out.

"Timmy will have Spitfire ready. You just do exactly as they say."

"What a pity! I have to ride Spitfire around the track a few times. This part is real hard to take." Trish reached back inside to grab her script off the seat. *"This* is the part I'm worried about." Worried didn't begin to cover it. The thought of saying lines already written and getting the right inflections turned her mouth to sawdust and her stomach to mush. Or tied it up in knots—whatever.

They crossed the gravel and stopped in front of a door on a tan trailer. The sign said Wardrobe/Makeup. Trish turned to look at Amy, who stepped forward and opened the door.

"After you."

"Hi, I'm Lennie." A young woman with skin the color of rich milk chocolate turned from the mirror where she'd been applying gloss to lips already lined with deep burgundy lipstick. "You must be Trish. Sit here and let's have a look at you." She gestured to the chair in front of the three-sided mirror bordered with lights that showed every pore and lash.

Trish did as she was told. "Guess I'm in your hands."

"Then you don't need to worry, honey. I've been doing this for ten years now." Lennie, rump perched on the edge of the makeup counter, studied her project carefully. "Hmmm." She tipped Trish's chin up and from side to side. "Joseph was right. The hair is glorious. With eyes like yours, no wonder the camera loves you. Good skin . . . those cheekbones will leap out with blusher . . . we'll narrow that nose a bit."

Trish now knew what dissection felt like. By the time Lennie was finished with her, she'd been pasted, powdered, and painted. Her hair had been braided loosely and her bangs fluffed to the side. But her eyes—they looked huge, and her lips—well, she grinned to see what she'd look like. Not bad. She glanced in the mirror to see Amy give her the thumbs-up sign.

"Ready in five." A knock sounded along with the voice.

"Now, you just go out there and wow 'em." Lennie handed Trish her helmet.

Spitfire nickered as soon as she stepped out the door. But when she tried to whistle, her mouth refused. Too dry to pucker. That along with the butterflies who awoke with the sun and now cavorted around her middle and Trish thought of the rain and cold at Portland Meadows with longing.

"Easy, fella." She rubbed cold fingers up behind his ears. "At least you're warm." But when she stepped forward to hug him, Joseph appeared at her shoulder.

"Don't let him get your silks dirty." He pushed back his Detroit Tigers ball cap and checked something on his clipboard. "If you'll mount now, we'll get under way. All I'd like you to do is run him around the track."

"How fast?"

"Well, like you're racing. You know that butt-in-the-air, hunched-forward look. And fast enough so his mane blows. The camera crew will be shooting from different locations so you needn't think about them. But do look like you're having a good time."

"I'm always having a good time on my friend here." Just as she turned to mount, Spitfire raised his nose with lightning speed and tipped the cap off the man's head.

Trish bit her lip. Hard. "Spitfire, no! Sorry. He thinks hats are a game."

Joseph reached down and, after dusting off his cap, put it back on his head, at the same moment taking two steps backward. "Remind me to watch out for him. Does he bite too?"

"No, only Gatesby does that."

"Gatesby?" He stared at her over the tops of the half-glasses he wore far down on his nose.

Trish stroked Spitfire's nose and kept her face straight. "He's a horse we train. You gotta watch him."

"And him." Joseph pointed at Spitfire with the end of his pen. "Horses with a sense of humor." He shook his head. "You learn something new everyday." He started to leave but turned back. "You didn't command him to do that, did you?"

"No. No way. I try to keep him honest."

"Just make sure you do."

Once on the track, thoughts of commercials and cameras left her mind completely. She drew in a breath of crisp fall air through her nose and let it out. "Well, Spitfire, old fella, this is your chance. Let's show 'em how beautiful you really are." She brought up her knees and found her stirrups. At the signal from Joseph she broke her mount into a canter and then a gallop. *Butt in the air, my foot.* She thought back to the producer's instructions. "Come on, fella, let's go."

Twice around the track and the signal came to stop. She pulled the colt down to a trot and then a walk. "Timmy was right. You're in good shape, old man." She stroked down the glistening hide. Barely warm.

"Okay, Trish, take a breather." Joseph gathered his camera people about him. Lennie came over to see if Trish needed any touch-ups but kept her distance from Spitfire.

"I never did trust anything bigger than me, honey. So don't you go taking offense. You look fine, anyway."

"Thanks. You seen Amy?"

"She's over talking to a good-looking redheaded young man."

"Red's here?"

"Guess that might be his name." She winked at Trish and marched back to her trailer.

"You want me to hold him?" Timmy asked, walking along at her right knee.

"No thanks, we're fine." She scanned the groups of people milling around. No blond Amy with a redheaded fellow. Then she saw an arm raised and waving.

"Trish!" Red broke away from the group and trotted across the gravel. "Sorry, I didn't realize you were on break." He walked the last few yards and, taking Spitfire's reins with one hand, reached the other up for Trish's. "You two look mighty fine out there." He squeezed her hand. "I am so glad to see you." His sky blue eyes said the rest.

"Can you believe we're doing this?" Her hand in his sent electric jolts clear to her toes. She leaned forward. "Can you believe they're paying me to ride my favorite horse in all the world?"

"I know. Rough life. Wish I could be out there with you."

"Okay, Trish, let's do the same again." This time Joseph stopped a few paces back. "We've clouds coming up from the west, so our sun might not last much longer."

Trish touched her gloved hand to her forehead. "Yes, sir," and nudged Spitfire forward. Red walked beside her knee. "I hear you've been having some trouble again."

"Amy blabbed." His comment snatched her thoughts

of The Jerk from their hiding place and displayed them front and center. "Thanks for nothing."

"Sorry. I didn't realize it was so bad." He shook his head. "No wonder David was so worried."

"David? How'd you know?"

"You ever heard of the U.S. mail? Or maybe it doesn't go to Washington yet. Couldn't prove it by the amount I've received, that's for sure."

Trish patted him on the head. "Sorry. Been a lot on my mind."

"If I could get my hands on him . . ."

"You and about a million others. Amy said they'd get him. He has to make a mistake one of these days. And maybe with me gone, he'll forget all about it."

"What are you waiting for, Trish?" The voice came over a bullhorn.

"Sorry, gotta go." She glanced to the west. Black thunderheads rose behind the trees, darkening the sky and sending a cold wind to bite Trish's nose and cheeks. "Looks like we may get wet. That'll send 'em into a tizzy for sure." She nudged Spitfire to a trot and then a gallop. The sun had melted the ground mist and now sparkled through the flaming leaves on the elm trees along the track.

Trish sniffed the air. Perfume of horse and burning leaves somewhere. What a combination. But after two more laps, they signaled her in.

"We'll move into the barn for the interior shots next. You can put your horse away for a while. It'll take us some time to get set up." Joseph signaled someone else toward the stallion barn. "Oh, and, Trish. You'll do these next shots with your hair down, so get back to makeup."

"Guess his mother never taught him to say please or

thank you," Trish muttered while she leaped to the ground and looked around for Timmy. Now she had to review her lines again. Her butterflies all fluttered at once—but not in rhythm.

An hour and a half later, the interior was finally set. Directly in front of Spitfire's stall sat a red LeBaron convertible, just like the one Trish drove at home. When it wasn't in the shop, that is.

All she had to do was hold Spitfire by the reins and stand with her hand on the car door. Besides saying her lines, of course.

After three dry runs, her mouth felt like the Sahara Desert. She hadn't said the words right any time.

Spitfire nudged her in the back as if to say, "Get with the program. I'm bored."

"Knock it off," she ordered under her breath.

"Okay, Lennie, get her some more mouth. And her forehead's getting shiny."

Timmy took Spitfire and walked him down the aisle while Trish stood still for more painting.

"You can do it, honey," Lennie murmured while dusting Trish's forehead. "Just relax."

Trish nodded. "Thanks."

Timmy brought Spitfire back and they started again. *Please, God, this is so new*. She took a deep breath. Spitfire snuffled her cheek. "Racing Spitfire is like riding the wind." She stepped forward. "So's driving my LeBaron."

Thunder crashed so hard the roof rattled.

Spitfire reared back, jerking the reins from her hands.

CHAPTER THIRTEEN

"Cut!"

"Easy, fella." Trish focused all her attention on her quivering horse. "It was just thunder. You've heard it plenty of times living back here." Spitfire leaned his forehead against her chest, letting her rub his ears and down his cheeks. "You're okay, you really are."

"Easy, son." Red joined Trish, with one hand smoothing Spitfire's shoulder, the other locked on a rein. "You're doin' fine."

"Trish, are you all right?" Joseph stopped just beyond Spitfire's reach. "Looked like he jerked your arm right out of the socket."

"No, I'm fine. You kinda learn to go with a horse when he freaks like that. Besides, Spitfire wouldn't hurt me, would you, fella?" She kept up her stroking. "He's really just a big baby, you know."

"Not intentionally anyway," Red muttered, all the while keeping his hands busy calming the colt.

"Right." Joseph didn't look as if he believed her for one minute.

"Hang on to him, Trish. Here comes another one."

151

Timmy appeared beside her and snapped a lead line onto the D ring of the bit. "That last one hit right above the barn."

Trish commanded her own body not to flinch with one side of her brain while comforting Spitfire with the other. She didn't like loud noises any better than he did.

Blue-white light flashed in the windows at the same moment as they heard a skull-vibrating crack. When the thunder kaboomed at the same instant, Trish kept a loose hold on the rein in case Spitfire reared again. She couldn't help the flinch. It sounded like something monstrous crashing into the barn roof.

Spitfire half reared again, one of his flailing front feet nicking the convertible door on his way back down. Feet back flat on the floor, he trembled from nose to tail.

But unlike thunder, the horrible sound kept on crashing. With metal screeching and booming, it sounded as if the entire world were falling and crumbling.

Spitfire stood with his head against Trish, his shiny black hide breaking out into darker patches of sweat. Timmy stood on the colt's offside, offering the same comfort as Trish.

"A tree fell on the wardrobe trailer!" one of the grips yelled from the doorway. "And two of the trucks. You won't believe the mess out here."

In spite of the pouring rain, everyone but the three with Spitfire dashed outside to see the damage. Trish looked down at her silks, now sprinkled with black hairs. "All the rest of my gear was in that trailer. This is the only set I have left."

"That's the least of our worries." Amy came to stand beside her after looking out the door. "Wait 'til you see the destruction out there." She joined Trish in stroking Spitfire. "I've never in my life seen rain like that. You can barely see the crashed tree and it's not a hundred feet away."

"Probably should just put him back." Lightning flashed again and Trish counted the seconds before the thunder boomed. "Two, three, four. It's passed us and going away."

"What were you doing?" Amy asked.

"Light travels faster than sound so when you count between the light and the sound, you can tell how far away the lightning flashed."

"Remind me how grateful I am we hardly ever have thunder and lightning storms in Washington. I didn't want to know all this."

Trish led Spitfire away from the convertible and down the aisle between stallion boxes, Timmy and Red keeping pace. Other stallions hung their heads over the web gates and either nickered or laid their ears back. Spitfire ignored them all, whuffling in her ear and nosing her pockets. Now that the rain no longer sounded like artillery fire on the roof, he barely twitched when more thunder rolled.

"He's been pretty good about the noises like that up to now," Timmy said, bringing the colt a handful of carrot pieces. "Just those two struck right here. I doubt they'll do any more shooting today."

"Great. And I never did get my lines right. This could take forever." Trish rubbed the side of her face against Spitfire's cheek. "I don't think I'm cut out to be a model, do you?"

By evening the crew had cut away the tree, brought in new trailers, and salvaged what they could from the damage. Trish's silks had only needed laundering, which she did up at the house. Lennie made a trip to Lexington to pick up new makeup to replace what was smashed, while one of the crew jerry-rigged a makeup mirror and counter for her to work at. Fortunately the tree had fallen toward the end of the trailer, rather than in the middle.

"We'll start again right after supper," Joseph announced about five o'clock. "Trish, think you could have your lines down by then?"

"I have them now." She flashed a look of gratitude at Red. They'd been rehearsing for hours. "I never dreamed this could be such work. Three stupid lines and I keep flubbing 'em," she muttered for his ears alone.

"I'd rather take a fall on the track than this." Red spoke in the same low tone. The smile he sent her warmed her middle. How come when she was with him, she felt all warm and fuzzy, but when she got home again, everything else took over and she only thought of him at night when she included him in her prayers or . . . She tried to think back. Nope, she didn't think of him every day during the day.

Someone else said something to him, so when he turned away, Trish studied his face. Intense blue eyes, a smile that warmed everyone in reach, square jaw, and wavy hair nearly the same carrot as Rhonda's. In fact, the two of them could pass for brother and sister. He laughed and answered another question about racing.

His laugh brought a smile to her face. One couldn't be down when Red was around. Could they be more than friends? Did she really want a boyfriend? Maybe this long-distance, half-off, half-on sorta romance was the best kind. She fingered the filigreed gold cross she always wore on a slim gold chain around her neck. Red had given her the gift after she won the Kentucky Derby.

His attention shifted back to her, his gaze telling her she was special. Trish couldn't break away; it was like a steel cable bound them together.

"That's the look I want on film." Joseph stopped beside them. "When the two of you are arguing over red or black. That look—pure sex appeal."

Trish blinked and felt the red flare up her neck and over her face, painting her in sheets of heat. "Why did I ever agree to do this?" she muttered to herself. "Why in the world do athletes want to do endorsements anyway?"

"For the money, silly." Amy answered from Trish's other side. Her comment made Trish realize she'd spoken her question aloud.

"Think about it," Red joined in. "With what you make from this you could bid on a yearling or buy a new broodmare."

Trish nodded. "That's right. Help me keep this in perspective. Otherwise I'm afraid when I get in front of those cameras again, I'm going to melt right into a puddle and drain through the floor."

"Come on, you were having a good time up there." Amy poked Trish in the side.

"Right. And you like getting shot at."

"Well, the adrenaline does give one a high."

Trish chewed on her bottom lip. "Speaking of adrenaline, you talk to Parks lately?"

"Last night, and he said to tell you no news is good news."

"But no leads yet?"

Amy put on her official look. "Ma'am, as to that, I'm

not at liberty to say." She grinned and shattered the image. "But at least The Jerk's not bugging you."

"How would he know where she is?" Red leaned forward so he could see Amy better.

"The press." Amy gave a sigh that spoke volumes. "You can bet Curt Donovan and his cohorts have let the entire world know Trish has this contract. Chrysler would have sent out press releases too. Trish, you just don't seem to understand. You are big news."

"I don't watch it or read it unless someone reminds me. Press doesn't really matter—it's doing your best that counts."

"I'll remind you of that the next time your agent has to turn away mounts." Red glanced up when someone called their names. "Let's go eat. We can continue this discussion later."

As if I want to. Trish rose to her feet.

By ten that night everyone's tempers danced like sparks from bare wires touching. Spitfire reacted to the tension and shifted from foot to foot, tossing his head and even laying his ears back. Trish felt she could do nothing right, and by now the car had a second ding in it from one of the colt's more determined protests.

Joseph finally threw up his hands and shut the entire process down. "Get some sleep and we'll start again at seven. Trish, it's coming, so don't tear yourself down. You learn really quickly for someone who's never done this before. Besides, working with animals is always difficult."

Trish stared at him, total disbelief mirrored on her face.

"Believe him, honey," Lennie whispered when she

took the silks and helmet off to wardrobe. "He doesn't pass out compliments lightly."

Even so Trish fell into bed wishing she were at any track in the world other than here. Freezing rain in Portland, or even taking a fall seemed preferable. Coming in last—well, not quite. She did hate to lose. She mumbled her three thank-yous and fell into the sleep of total exhaustion.

"Heavenly Father, please get me through this day." She whispered the plea before getting out of bed in the morning. "I can't do this without your help. I'm not a model or an actress. I'm a jockey." She rolled her head to the side. Outside the window was still pitch black. But she'd already shut off the alarm, so she had to get going. "I can do all things through Him who strengthens me." She repeated the verse three times. Her "amen" was echoed by a rooster crowing.

"Rise and shine." Amy tapped on the door. "Meet you downstairs."

"All right." Trish threw back the covers. The rooster crowed again, sending his wake-up call echoing over the treetops. "All right, I said I was coming." Trish headed for the bathroom. She could get used to having her own private bath. She could get used to a lot of the things here at BlueMist.

Her heels clicking down the stairs, she caught herself humming the opening bars to her song. She needed some eagle's wings today for sure.

"We're all praying for you, Tee." Marge sat down at the breakfast table next to her daughter. "I watched for a while last night but I finally left. Joseph gives new meaning to the word perfectionist."

"At least he liked the clips of me riding Spitfire. That storm yesterday sent everything crazy."

"I just thank God no one was hurt. And a fire didn't start."

"A fire would have had a hard time of it with all that pouring rain." Trish drained her glass of milk and pushed back her chair. "See ya, Mom. Gotta go to work."

On the third take, she finally pulled everything together: lines, looks, and Spitfire's ears pointing in the right direction. "Cut and that's a wrap. Good job, Trish, and give that black beast an extra carrot." Joseph pushed his hat farther back on his head and stretched his arms in front of him. "Okay, everyone, back after dinner. We'll be outside again."

They spent the afternoon rehearsing Trish and Red together without the horse. By dusk Trish felt if she had to say the lines one more time, smile one more time, or stroke that stupid car, she'd bust out screaming.

"No wonder models get paid a bunch of money. This is the worst job I've ever had." She glanced over at Red, who was shrugging his shoulders up to his ears to loosen the kinks.

"You ever washed dishes in a restaurant?" Amy asked. "Now that's bad. I put myself through college working in a restaurant, starting with dishwasher. Thought I'd died and gone to heaven when I finally made waitress, and that's no easy job either."

Trish shrugged off the twinge of guilt. "Does mucking out stalls count?"

"We've gotta get this right tomorrow. I have four mounts on Thursday at Churchill Downs."

"And the weather has to cooperate." Amy raised her

face to the evening breeze. "You sure can tell fall is in the air."

The three of them marched up the steps of the big house. Smells to tempt angels wafted out from the kitchen. Sarah had been hard at it, they could tell.

———————

When morning came, it brought a fine mist.

"Weatherman says sun this afternoon, so you two keep at it." Joseph tapped his pen on his clipboard. "I want you back in the barn at ten, Trish. There's one spot we need to reshoot. Won't take long."

But it did. And the sun didn't come out till late afternoon, leaving too-long shadows and too little time with light. Joseph was counting on the sun glimmering through the trees.

Trish could feel Red's tension when they walked back up to the house. "I'm sorry." She didn't know what else to say.

"It's not your fault." He shoved his hands in his pockets. "Guess I better just call my agent and get it over with. Here I thought I could work it all in."

"I know. I hate letting owners and trainers down too and I haven't been winning consistently like you. Donald says you're going to be a force to reckon with in a couple of years if you keep going like you are."

"Thanks for trying, Trish. I'll see you later."

Bernice met Trish and Amy at the door. "Trish, there's some mail for you. It's on the table in the parlor."

CHAPTER FOURTEEN

Trish felt her stomach bounce on her kneecaps.

"I'll get it." Amy shifted into police mode from one breath to another. "You stay here."

"Is there a problem?" Bernice stared from Trish to Amy, her hand to her mouth. "Oh, no, that's why you're with Trish, isn't it—letters just like this."

"Just pray that's all it is." Amy said, her heels clicking out her concern as she crossed the hardwood floor.

Trish followed Amy into the antique-furnished parlor but stopped at the doorway. She didn't really want to see the thing. But then it could be from Rhonda or David or . . .

Amy muttered a word that told Trish her bodyguard's state of mind. For sure the letter wasn't an "I'm thinking of you" card.

"Let me see it." Trish stiffened her spine along with her knees and crossed the room. Amy held the plain white paper by the corner. "Good luck," the block letters read. "Did you think you could run away from me?"

Trish's stomach took another knee dive.

"You go eat. I have some phone calls to make."

"Since Red is on the line in Donald's office, you can use the home phone." Bernice pointed to one set on a carved-walnut whatnot table beside a deep leather chair. "We'll leave you alone." She put an arm around Trish's shoulders. "Come, dear. Let's join the others in the dining room."

Trish let herself be led out of the room. They met Red coming out of the office. He took one look at Trish's face.

"What happened now?"

"Another letter." Bernice locked her other arm through his and drew them both forward. "We can discuss this over Sarah's baked ham. Stewing about it won't make one whit of difference. That's a job for the police."

So will he show up at the track? Come here to BlueMist? Trish slapped a lid on her thoughts and took her place at the table. When Red held the chair for her, he laid a comforting hand on her shoulder, gave a gentle squeeze, and then seated Marge.

Trish flashed him a look of pure gratitude. "Guess I've been having too good a time. Seemed like I was safe here."

"Yeah, in between rearing horses, lightning, falling trees, and a director who can shoot daggers at ten paces, it's real safe here." Red sat down on Trish's other side.

"Better all that than a harassing letter."

"You just forget all your troubles and enjoy my ham and yams." Sarah set the platter of biscuits directly in front of Trish. "There ain't nothin' that a good Southern meal can't cure, child. You eat up and see."

Trish smiled up at the woman serving. One could never resist smiling with Sarah. "I suppose you baked pies again today."

"No, honey, I made apple cobbler. Wait 'til you try it."

She bustled back out after giving Trish's shoulder a second pat.

Donald said grace and began serving the plates from the platters in front of him. As usual, there was enough to feed each of them three times and still have leftovers.

"I'm going to have to go on a diet when I get home, and I never have to diet." Trish bit into a piece of ham. She'd take Sarah's advice. Let the food do its work and Officer Parks do his.

"I do. And after a meal like this, I should run ten miles. But I'm always too full." Red forked another bite of ham into his mouth and closed his eyes in appreciation.

The next day's shooting took off from the first frame and stopped only for meals.

"You're doing it, kids," Joseph said at one point. "That's just the look I want."

Trish grinned at Red and hugged Spitfire, who acted like he'd been on camera all his life and what was all the fuss about? Maybe the modeling stuff wasn't so bad after all.

They took their places for the umpteenth time. They stood together between the two convertibles—one black, one red, front bumpers nearly touching.

"Okay, roll it."

"Red is best." Trish looked up at Red from under her eyelashes.

"Nope, black." His half-grin sent a shiver up her back.

"Either way, we'll take LeBarons." The words came out slowly, as if they'd been drenched in warm honey.

Trish couldn't take her gaze from his mouth, his smiling, curved lips so near.

"Cut! That's it! Talk about sizzle."

Trish blinked. Spitfire nudged her for attention. The mood shattered.

"Okay, let's set up for the next shots."

No matter how well it went, it was still ten o'clock that night before they finished. Trish had heard a phrase once—"drug through a knothole backwards." Now she knew what it meant. And how it felt. They had to leave for Churchill Downs by seven in the morning.

Red dropped a kiss on the end of her tired nose and left as soon as they finished shooting. He had horses to ride for morning works. The thought of riding five or six mounts before seven and most likely freezing in the process made Trish shiver in sympathy.

She would enjoy her vacation just a little longer. If what she'd been doing could be called a vacation, that is.

She gave a halfhearted thought to her books, the ones she'd carted so faithfully across the country. She'd been studying all right, but lines, not textbooks. Maybe she could write a term paper on the joys of modeling. Trish groaned at the thought. Was there any chance her teachers would give her an extension?

One thought of The Jerk flitted through her mind, but there was a good side to exhaustion—she was too tired to care.

The sun didn't bother to get up early in the morning and when it did, it dressed in gray clouds rather than golden beams. She'd slept right through her rooster alarm so had to hustle. She would take a shower at the track.

Trish gave a last longing look around her bedroom. Since Marge and Bernice were driving over later, they would pack and bring her clothes. She hefted her sports bag and tried not to clatter down the stairs.

Sarah met her with a food package at the door. "Land sakes, child! Y'all can't go off for a big day like this on an empty stomach."

A horn honked from the drive. "Gotta run." Trish took the gift and planted a kiss on the woman's dark cheek. "Anytime you want to move west, let us know. Thanks for everything."

"I'll see you at the track this afternoon. Wouldn't miss it for the world."

With the warmth of a last pat still on her cheek, Trish dashed out the door and down the steps.

"I was beginning to think I was going to have to come haul you out of bed." Amy opened the door to the shiny deep blue Cherokee. "As usual, we're going in style."

Trish munched her breakfast, letting the conversation flow around her. Traveling with either of the Shipsons was a touring lesson in history, done in a most entertaining style. She could tell Amy was as charmed as she was.

The first sight of the three cupolas on the rooftops of Churchill Downs always brought a lump to her throat. "Far cry from Portland Meadows, right?" She turned around when Amy failed to answer. If one's face could register shock, Amy's did. Mouth open, eyes wide. Yup, shock for sure. Trish felt a chuckle coming on. In spite of the low gray sky, this was going to be a super day. Wasn't it? But a niggle of fear set her butterflies a-fluttering.

"You all right?" Amy recovered enough to sense the change in Trish.

"Sure. Fine." But Trish caught herself carefully studying each person they drove by, just in case they might be *the* one.

So much for trust and faith, Nagger whispered in her ear. *You claim God will take care of you, now let Him.* Trish breathed deeply to relax. And it helped, in spite of the fact that increased oxygen accelerated the butterfly acrobatics.

She was all right. Of course she was. Here at Churchill Downs she could be no other.

The first face she saw when they reached the Shipsons' barn belonged to her California trainer, Adam Finley. Trish leaped from the truck and flew into his arms.

"Hey, it's been worth the wait for a greeting like that. Let me look at you, now a world-class model no less. You have more talents than one person should know what to do with." A smile wreathed his face like the white fringe of hair circled his shiny bald crown.

"Right. You been kissing the Blarney stone or something?" Trish hooked her arm in his. "Come meet my friend Amy and then I get to inspect the string."

"Inspection, my foot. Firefly thought you were coming to take her out this morning. She's been pining for you."

"Sure she has. I bet she gave that redheaded friend of ours a good workout." Trish introduced Amy and Adam, then grabbed Amy's arm. "You met the humans—now come see the important people around here."

Firefly had stretched her head so far out of the stall she looked as if she might topple over. Her nickers demanded attention, giving vent to a full-fledged whinny when Trish didn't respond quickly enough.

"You silly girl, I think you missed me." Trish handed Amy a piece of carrot. "Here, this sweetie will be your friend for life if you come with treats in hand. I should know."

"Right, you're the one who spoiled her rotten." Adam stood petting the gelding in the stall next to the filly so he wouldn't feel left out. "This is your other mount for today. He's looking mighty fine here—clocked out well."

Trish switched horses. "He does look good."

Amy stood next to Firefly's shoulder, stroking the red-gold hide and adopting Trish's habit of crooning sweet nothings into the filly's twitching ears.

"You're turning into a real horse person," Trish said.

"I think I've always been one. That side of me just got put on hold, that's all. You think Kevin would mind me having a horse?"

"How should I know? He's *your* fiancé. I haven't even met him yet." Trish left off with her filly and followed Donald Shipson down the line of curious horses.

"This is your mount for the second race. You've ridden him before, and he's improved a lot since then. By the way, you'll be riding against Red in all three races."

"That should make for more fun. I love beating out my friends."

"You better head up to the jockey room." Donald checked his watch. "You know how strict they are about check-in times."

Trish waved to Amy. "Come on, buddy. We gotta get going."

By the time they'd walked around the track, thunderheads reared above the skyline. Trish could see lightning flashing in the distance and hear the thunder muttering.

"Will they race even if it storms?"

"This track is so well maintained that it can handle a lot of water and still be dry enough to race. Sometimes they delay between squalls, though."

Trish tried to study while they waited for the program to begin, but she felt so restless she could hardly sit still. Up and down she paced, into the lounge between the men's and women's jockey rooms, where jockeys played cards or shot pool or just shot the breeze. She bought a Diet Coke and visited with Red. Then back to her books. What was wrong with her?

"Good luck." She gave Red a thumbs-up sign when he headed out for the first race. And when he won it, she went nuts along with the others. It was easy to tell he was a favorite in the women's dressing room, for sure.

When the call came for the second race, they took the escalator down and walked out the jockey passage together. While Trish heard her name cheered a couple of times, Red again seemed to be a special favorite of the crowd. She could tell why—his ready smile helped everyone enjoy their day.

Her butterflies lodged in a traffic jam, right in her throat. Donald Shipson gave her a leg up and an encouraging smile. "This is just a race, like any other. No big deal."

Trish's smile helped relax her entire body. "How come you always have just the right words to make people feel better?"

"It's a gift. Now, this old boy likes to set the pace, but he can't today because Red will run you right into the ground if you let him." At Trish's nod, he continued.

"And he needs the whip to kick into the sprint, so don't hesitate to use it."

The bugle rose above the tall green roof of the stands and floated back down to the paddock. Donald handed her off to the pony rider, and out the tunnel under the stands they walked.

While the gelding strutted his stuff for the crowd, Trish glanced at the grandstand. This was nothing like Derby day, when every seat was taken and the infield was full. And now, spectators huddled in blankets.

Red saluted her with his whip from three horses over when the horses entered the starting gates. Trish nodded back.

At the gun they broke clear. Trish forgot all but the horse she rode and the finish line six furlongs away. "Easy, fella," she sang through the first turn. She looked to the right to see Red hanging even with her. Two horses ahead dueled for the lead. But out of the turn, she went to the whip just like Shipson said. Within strides she and Red had left the two front runners behind and drove nose to nose for the swiftly approaching tall white posts.

"Come on!" Trish swung her whip again, two right-handed slaps. The gelding leaped forward. Two strides and he crossed the line. A win by a nose. Trish grinned at Red and flashed him a victory sign. "Sorry about that," she called.

"Sure you are. My turn next."

"Good job, Trish. You rode that one perfectly." Shipson, Bernice, and Marge joined Trish in the winner's circle. "I'll bet Red wishes you'd stayed in Washington."

"Oh, I don't think so, dear," Bernice drawled, making them all laugh.

The next race could have been a rerun except for a

different ending. Red gave the victory signal and Trish
took the place.

"Sorry, Adam. I tried, I really did." Trish jumped to
the ground.

"I'm happy with this. Winning would have been
good, but this old boy did just fine." He let the groom
lead the gray gelding away. "You be ready now. Firefly's
waiting."

Trish nodded and headed back up the stairs to the
jockey room. She had four races to wait out.

By the seventh race the rain still held off except for
a sprinkle now and then. But when Trish followed the
line of jockeys out to the saddling paddock, it looked like
a mighty hand had painted the sky black.

"Sure hope this holds off a few more minutes. I don't
like the look of those clouds at all." Adam rebuckled the
girth and checked the fit on the bridle. "You know this
girl better than anyone, Trish. You need to watch numbers four and eight. I think they're the real contenders."

Trish nodded her agreement. Her mouth had
adopted the Sahara feel again. Thunder clapped and she
flinched. *Knock it off*, she ordered herself. *You know how
to relax, so just do it*. She smoothed her fingers down the
bright white number one. She hated being on the rail.
Firefly didn't care for it much either. Guess they'd just
have to break faster than anyone.

Totally calm on the outside and fluttering on the inside, Trish waited for the gun. At the shot, the gates
clanged open and Firefly leaped out in a perfect break.

"Easy, girl." Trish kept a firm hand on the reins but
let the filly set her own pace. Going through the turn
they pulled ahead enough to let Firefly run the way she
liked. Down the backstretch they pounded, horses jock-

eying for position. Into the final turn. Lightning flashed just above the cantilevered roof of the grandstands, seeming to dance on the third cupola. The heavens opened like a dam sending water thundering down a river.

The riders and horses were drenched between one breath and the next. The horse who came up on the outside faltered and clipped Firefly's rear foot. Trish heard a crack. Firefly fell forward and Trish catapulted over the filly's head.

The force when she hit the ground came from both sides. She tried to roll as she'd been taught, but a weight crushed down on her chest. When Trish forced her eyes open to a slit, Firefly stood with one foreleg dangling. *Not Firefly!* Her silent scream followed her down the deep black pit of oblivion.

When she felt the medics putting her on a board, she came to enough to mumble, "Don't let them put her down."

"Easy, miss." A rich Southern voice tried to calm her.

"No!" Trish summoned every bit of strength she had. She heard Adam's voice somewhere near. "Promise! Adam! Don't put her down!"

"I'll try, Tee. As God is my witness, I'll try."

The blackness surged back.

———————

Trish could hear her mother's voice, but no matter how hard she tried, no words made it out of her mind. Marge was praying; that much Trish knew. The medical people made several comments as they worked over her. *I must be hurt bad this time.* The thought floated through her mind. She didn't have any ability to stop it. But thoughts were all she could manage.

She heard doctors giving sharp commands and the words "surgery—stat!" along with "punctured lung." *Must be pretty serious.* The words "code blue" shocked her. What shocked her even more was her point of view. Trish felt as if she were floating up in the corner of the room, looking down on the table where the surgical team worked over a body. Was that *her* down there? And if so, what was she doing up here? *Am I dreaming? If I am, this is the strangest dream I've ever had.*

She felt herself drifting off when suddenly a long dark tunnel beckoned, and with a mild sense of curiosity, she entered it. Far away at the end, it appeared as if a light were guiding her. Total peace surrounded her. In fact, she seemed to float on a current drawing her closer with love. She followed the light, her curiosity deepening. Just when she felt sure she would see someone she knew, she felt snapped backward like a ball on the end of a rubber band.

The doctor's voice sounded above her. "Okay, we got her. Let's get this stitched up and get outa here." Trish heard no more.

When she floated back up out of the gray swirling clouds, she could hear her mother talking with a gentle-sounding woman. Trish felt her eyelids flutter open, as if the action helped pull her mind back to the room.

"You're awake." Marge leaned over the bed so Trish could see her without moving her head. Trish blinked her eyes. Nodding took too much effort.

Why didn't you let me stay there? But with the tracheal tube in her throat so she could breath, she couldn't say anything even if she'd had the strength.

"You're in intensive care. The doctors repaired your lung."

The accident came screaming back. A shudder started at her feet and raced upward.

"Tee, it's okay. You're going to be fine." A tear trickled down Marge's cheek. "You're going to be fine."

What about Firefly? But Trish slipped back into fog, unable to ask her question.

When she swam to the surface the next time, David stood next to the bed, holding her hand. Maybe it was his voice that woke her up. "Hi, baby sister. Now don't panic, easy. Firefly is in about the same shape you are." As the tension eased out of Trish's jaw, he smiled again. "I knew that's what was worrying you. There's a plate and a bunch of screws in her leg, so if it heals right, we'll be able to use her for a broodmare, at least."

Trish felt ten-pound weights pulling her eyelids back down, and she was off to the swirls where there was no noise, no pain, nothing. If only she could stay awake long enough to tell them about the bright place.

Pain like nothing she'd known in her life brought her back to reality. *Leave me alone!* While the words screamed in her mind, only a groan escaped around the tube.

"Hey, welcome back." The nurse at Trish's head smiled down at her. "I know this is making you uncomfortable, but you're on your way to a regular room."

Uncomfortable! Lady . . . Trish clamped her teeth together, but all they hit was the tube.

"On three." They lifted her from one bed to another with a sheet just like she'd moved Caesar on the tarp. Trish escaped back into the world of nothing.

"Water." Trish's eyes flew open. She'd actually said a

word. No tube. Oxygen by nose prongs. Bed in a room with peach color on the walls.

"Here." Marge pressed a spoon against Trish's lips. "It's ice for you to suck on. It'll help the thirst."

Trish took the wonderful cold chips in her mouth and let them lie on her tongue. She'd never appreciated ice before. Better than—"Can I have a Diet Coke?" Her croak could only have been heard in a silent room.

David laughed from the foot of the bed. "She's getting better." He came up and took her hand. "That's my sister."

Trish accepted more ice chips. When she tried to move, pain shot through her from front to back and around. Maybe it was chickening out to sleep, but it didn't hurt there. When would she be able to tell them about her adventure?

"The doctors said we almost lost you." It was the next day, and with Trish able to talk better, Marge sat filling in some holes for her questioning daughter.

"I know. I heard them." Trish turned her head to be able to look right at her mother. "Mom, it was the neatest thing. Like I was watching what they were doing, watching from up in the corner of the ceiling. Then I saw this long tunnel with a light way at the other end and when I started down it, I wasn't afraid. It was full of peace. When I got to the end, there was the most glorious light . . ."

Trish stopped, letting her mind remember and the rest of her feel.

"And then?" Marge whispered, tears streaming down her cheeks.

"I felt as if Dad was there but I didn't see him." Trish paused again. "I don't think he had a choice."

"A choice?"

"Uh-huh. I got to live. But I don't blame Dad for wanting to stay there. Such love. All around." Trish grasped her mother's hand. "It was beautiful!" She turned again to watch her mother's face. "Don't cry. I'm here." Trish's lips curved in a smile. "This world's a pretty special place, isn't it?"

Marge nodded. "Yes, it is."

"Mom, I just got the strangest feeling. Would you pray with me for Kendall Highstreet?"

"Of course." Marge blinked before leaning closer to the bed. "You're ready for that?"

Trish nodded. "It's like I have to." They clasped hands together and let the silence of the room surround them. "Heavenly Father, please come into Highstreet's life. Help him to know you as Lord and Savior." She paused. "Your turn."

Marge added some requests of her own and closed with, "Thank you for bringing Trish back to me."

"I'm not afraid anymore. Everything looks different, brighter, shinier. Like you. . . . Did you know your face glows when you look at me?"

"Must be love, huh?" Marge wiped the tears from her cheeks.

"I think I got a miracle." Trish's voice contained the wonder that lit her face.

"Having you right here is miracle enough for me." Marge laid her hand along Trish's cheek. "Why don't you sleep now so you can get better fast?"

"Wonder what I had to come back for?" Her eyelids fluttered on her cheekbones.

"I'm sure God will let you know—in time." Marge raised Trish's hand and held it against her cheek.

"He will, won't He?" Trish smiled again and drifted off into the healing sleep her body needed.